DESERT
Places

by

Erica Abbott

Bella
BOOKS

2015

Editor: Katherine V. Forrest
Cover Designer: Judith Fellows

ISBN: 978-1-59493-457-5

Other Bella Books by Erica Abbott

Acquainted with the Night
Certain Dark Things
Fragmentary Blue
One Fine Day

Acknowledgments

Books can introduce us to people we would never otherwise meet and lives we shall never live. They also can take us to places we will never visit. While the cities and county where this book takes place are fictional, the land and the mountains are real and part of a rare and beautiful landscape of the high desert,

As always, I thank Linda Hill, Karin Kallmaker and the terrific staff at Bella Books for making this book possible. I must particularly thank my editor, Katherine V. Forrest, for her work in the delicate art of constructive criticism.

My friends and loved ones have been my guides, therapists and patient listeners and I am grateful for them every day. I would also like to mention the fine examples set by the law enforcement officers it has been my privilege to know over the years—they permit me to write characters inspired by their dedication.

About the Author

Erica Abbott has worked as a local government attorney and prosecutor, college professor and writer. She has been a singer, a fairly good bridge player and a fairly bad golfer. She also loves dogs, cats, all kinds of music and really good books. She lives in Colorado.

Dedication

To my love, always and forever
and for MJ

PROLOGUE

Jean saw the blood as soon as she opened the door to the house.

She ran down the hall, blood flowing like a warm scarlet river under her feet. When she burst through the open doorway to the master bedroom, she saw Charlotte sitting on the edge of their bed. Jean looked down to see bright red blood pouring out of a hole in the center of her chest where her heart should have been.

With dead eyes, Charlotte looked at Jean and said, "You see what you did to me?"

Jean woke with a jerk and the echo of a sharp cry.

The room was dark, lit only by the pale yellow ghosts of the streetlights two floors below. Jean sat up, heart throbbing in her chest. The T-shirt she slept in was damp with sweat and she plucked it away from her body.

It had been months since the last nightmare. What had brought it back now?

The move, she thought, that must be it. She'd changed everything, her job and her home, moving hundreds of miles away to a new life.

You can't get away from me. She heard the whisper in her mind.

Jean threw the bedcovers violently aside and got up. The wood floor was cold against the soles of her feet, reminding her that she still had a lot of things to buy for the condominium, including a rug for the bedroom. She padded barefoot into the kitchen, opening three cabinets in the dark before she remembered which one she'd put the glasses in. Groping for the water cooler, she filled the glass and drank it down thirstily. She refilled the glass and took it back into her bedroom.

Sitting on the edge of the bed, she pressed the cold glass to her forehead. Accustomed as she was to the humidity of Texas summers, the dry hot air of the high plains in southern Colorado still surprised her. It seemed impossible to drink enough water.

Her air-conditioning unit hummed, fighting to keep the bedroom cool, but Jean wasn't bothered by the heat. For what had seemed a long time her body was always frozen, as if beneath her skin was a layer of permafrost never touched by the sun.

She drank the rest of the water and got under the covers, hoping that the remainder of the night would bring her respite from the dreams.

CHAPTER ONE

"The boss wants to see you right away," Jean McAllister heard from her office doorway.

She looked up to see Rita Lopez, one of the paralegals in the San Carlos county attorney's office, waiting for her.

"Okay," Jean said quickly, turning her eyes back to her computer monitor. "Thanks, Rita."

Unwilling to be dismissed, Rita added, "He really needs to see you before the public hearing, he said."

Jean glanced at the time. The San Carlos county commissioners met at ten a.m. every Monday morning, which meant she had less than ten minutes to get down the hall and finish with the county attorney before he had to be in the meeting. With an unhappy sigh, she saved the document on her screen and got up.

"Thanks," Rita murmured as Jean passed her. "You know how he gets."

Rita's expression radiated relief and Jean just managed not to scowl at her, reminding herself that the summons from Del

Franklin wasn't Rita's fault. Jean had been the deputy county attorney, second in command in the office, for less than a month, but she already knew that her boss could be nasty when those around him didn't jump when he whistled.

The county attorney's office represented the board and county officials by providing legal advice and representing the county in court. Her boss had been appointed by the three elected members of the board of county commissioners and keeping them happy took up much of his time.

She thought about Del Franklin as she walked down the carpeted hall toward his office. He had seemed nice enough when she'd interviewed for the job, a bit forceful maybe, but then Jean herself could be more than a little intense. At the time she'd thought they might make a good pairing of co-workers but she was beginning to wonder.

Jean shook off her doubts as she knocked on the frame of Franklin's door. She was going to make a success of this job because she had to—there was no going back.

"Rita said you needed to see me?" she said when Franklin looked up.

"Where have you been, McAllister?" he demanded.

"In my office, working on the Speedy Auto Sales brief," Jean answered in a crisp voice.

Franklin had a face that had probably been good-looking when he was in college or law school. Now he had sandy hair that was going thin and large brown eyes that always seemed bloodshot. From this distance Jean saw the flushed cheeks and tiny broken blood vessels in his nose as signs of a man who drank every night. Franklin snapped, "Aren't you done with that yet? It's just a Rule 106 appeal."

Jean tried not to grit her teeth. A landowner who appealed an adverse zoning decision by the county board had to proceed under Civil Rule of Procedure 106 and was required to show that the board had no evidence to deny the rezoning. The standard for the landowner was almost impossible to meet and therefore counties won almost every appeal. In a larger office, such a case would have been assigned to a junior attorney, but

Jean understood that she would have a reasonable amount of grunt work to do with only five attorneys in the entire office.

"We still have to file a brief," Jean reminded him, trying to hide her own flare of annoyance. "And since I wasn't here when the case was heard, I had to review the entire case file and review the hearing transcript before I could start."

He snorted, apparently unhappy that he had no logical reason to criticize her further. He switched topics. "Look, I've got to get to the meeting with the board. I want you to get the Rosales file from Lopez. The discovery schedule on the case is about to bite us in the ass. We've got a deposition scheduled for next week that you need to cover."

Jean's eyes narrowed. "Are we taking the depo or defending?" she asked.

He stood impatiently. "Defending. They're finally getting around to deposing our sheriff and you'll need to do the prep."

Thanks for the advance notice. Jean counted to ten silently and then asked, "Is it my case or am I just defending the deposition for you?"

Franklin snatched up his file folder marked Sept. 13 BCC public hearing. He said, "It's your case now. After discovery closes, you'll need to do a Motion for Summary Judgment and see if we can beat the defendants down to a reasonable amount for the settlement."

She walked him into the hallway as she tried to pry a little more information from him. "What's the lawsuit about?" she asked. Most lawsuits against the county were either land use issues, like the rezoning case she was working on, or personal injury claims from accidents with public vehicles or on public roads. Because the county attorney's office didn't prosecute criminal matters, she would only represent the sheriff in a civil lawsuit.

"Some guy died in our jail," Franklin said. "Read the pleadings, McAllister. I've got to go."

He strutted off and Jean shook her head in irritation. A wrongful death action was a major suit and yet again she was being handed a case already halfway through.

It's going to be like this for a while, Jean told herself, *until I've been here long enough to start practicing some preventive law.*

She found Rita, who handed her a thick file folder labeled *Rosales v. San Carlos sheriff*. Jean stood by Rita's desk and flipped the file open. Everything was in the one file, attached to the folder with a double metal prong that was full. One more sheet of paper and the entire case file would fall apart in her hands.

"Rita, what's going on?" Jean snapped. "This file is a mess."

Rita glanced meaningfully toward Franklin's office then looked back to Jean. "He doesn't like us to organize his case files," she said apologetically. "He just puts everything in chronologically."

Jean looked at her aghast, remembering at the last second not to kill the messenger. "Yes, well he's assigned the case to me now, so I'd be an idiot not to use my paralegal, wouldn't I? This needs some serious attention right away. Pleadings in one folder, correspondence in another, discovery in another, you know the system. If you're not sure where something goes, ask me." She flipped through the pile of documents rapidly. "Any legal research in here, do you know?"

Rita shook her head. "I don't know. I'll reorganize the file myself. Deb hasn't had a lot of experience with the litigation files."

"Okay, but I need it as soon as possible. Apparently the plaintiff is deposing our sheriff next week and I've got to get him prepped right away."

"Her," Rita said.

Jean was already turning back toward her office while mentally organizing her schedule. Finish the Speedy Auto brief by this afternoon, file it electronically and then go through the Rosales file and—

"What?" she said to Rita, finally registering her comment.

"Her," Rita repeated. "Sheriff Lea Hawkins. Our sheriff is a woman."

Jean blinked at her. She'd tried to meet as many elected officials as she could, but the sheriff's office was in another building and she just hadn't had time yet.

"Okay," she said, still distracted. "I've got to prepare her for the deposition but I've got to read the file first, so the sooner you can get it to me the better."

"I'll have it for you by the end of the day," Rita promised.

Jean tried to make an effort. She needed the goodwill of the best paralegal in the office if she expected to get anything done and Rita had always been both pleasant and efficient. She was a pretty woman with dark hair she kept in a long ponytail. "Rita?" she said, managing a smile. "Thanks, I do appreciate it."

Rita returned a smile of her own. Jean wondered briefly how long it had been since Del Franklin had said something nice to her.

"No problem, Ms. McAllister."

* * *

Jean was checking her citations to case law as the last step in finishing the Speedy Auto brief when she heard another voice in her doorway.

"Um, Jean? Got a minute?"

Assistant county attorney Todd Moorman hovered in her doorway. Jean suppressed a sigh. Patiently she said, "Come in. I've got to finish the cite-checking on this real quick and send it to Rita and then I'm good."

She finished verifying that the citations to legal authority were all correct and then typed a quick email to Rita, asking her to format the brief and file it with the district court. Almost all court filings were done electronically, but the briefs still had to be in the correct format and the paralegals were the experts in e-filing.

Jean sat back and tried not to think about the pile of newly organized file folders on her desk that represented the Rosales case and her next task. She focused on Todd. "How are things going?"

"Um, okay, I think," Todd said. "I know you're busy."

Jean said, "Well, we're all busy. What's up?"

He rubbed his hands on the arms of the chair and she mentally tried to hurry him up. *Come on, I've got stuff to do here!* But she knew the harder she pressed him the more indirect he would become. Everything about Todd seemed tentative, from his unpolished brown shoes to his ties, which never looked like he quite knew how to knot them correctly.

Jean had a sudden brief and clear memory of tying Charlotte's ties for her, when Char was doing front of the house work at her restaurant. Char hated dealing with customers most of the time but she knew how to turn on the charm when called for, Jean remembered. But Char never could figure out a Windsor knot. Many times Jean would stand behind her and tie the black tie perfectly, a skill perfected when she had learned to tie her little brother's ties before Sunday school years before. Then Jean would kiss Char and tell her how nice she looked.

Will the random pieces of memory ever go away? Jean wondered. Or perhaps they would continue to pinball around her mind haphazardly for the rest of her life.

"I've got this case in front of the planning commission," Todd was saying, and as he talked Jean wondered why he was coming to her with this question. The planning commission was only a recommending body anyway since the board of county commissioners made the final land use decisions for the unincorporated parts of the county. More to the point, Todd had been in the county attorney's office three years already and Jean had to wonder what he thought she knew that he didn't.

Technically, of course, she was his supervisor, since Franklin had gladly turned over personnel management to her. It was one of the reasons she'd taken the job. Supervision of other attorneys and the staff was the next logical step in her government career and she was looking forward to the challenges of management. So far, personnel supervision had only been wrangling over time sheets and days off.

Todd was talking about the planning commission case, but she was listening with half her brain, the other part thinking about the Rosales case she'd just received. Defending a deposition, where the other side was asking most of the questions, wasn't as difficult as taking a depo, but the hard work took place beforehand. The witness had to be carefully prepared for the questions, and given the size of the case file, Jean suspected that the deposition was probably scheduled for a couple of days. She had to read the entire file, probably do some legal research and then spend hours prepping the sheriff. And she had less than a week to do it in. *God, I hope she's at least been deposed before or this is going to take forever.*

Todd was finishing with, "So I couldn't get them to reset the hearing to a date certain because the applicant wasn't sure when he could get the reports back from the water and sanitation district."

Jean waited. When he didn't continue, she asked, "So what's the issue?"

He fiddled with his tie, which was slightly askew as usual. "We have to republish all the notices, right?"

Oh, for God's sake. "Yes, Todd, you have to send out new letters to the interested parties and repost the property when the new date is set." She refrained from adding, *And any first-year assistant county attorney would know that.*

He nodded as if he really had known the answer all along. Jean stared at him, wondering for the first time if Todd had really meant to ask her something else. "Are you all right, Todd?" she asked.

He stood suddenly, as if he'd made a decision. "Yes, thanks," he said.

He was out of her office in a couple of seconds, almost trotting as if to escape.

Well, that was weird. The next moment she mentally dismissed Todd Moorman and pulled the pile of folders toward her.

* * *

Jean tossed her glasses on top of the nearest file and stretched her arms above her head. A glance outside told her that the sun had already set. Dusky shadows were darkening the county annex building across the street. The colors here were different than in Texas where she had grown up, or Southern California, where she'd been the last seventeen years. Texas was red clay and a damp heat that turned the sky hazy blue. The Coachella Valley was even hotter but the abundant water made it green and lush in the midst of the desert. San Carlos was warm and dry and every color of the earth, caramel and chocolate and toast.

She smiled to herself. *Okay, I'm obviously hungry.* She pushed the pile of folders away and reached for her keyboard to check her email.

She'd assigned Rita the task of trying to set a time for her to meet with sheriff Hawkins so she opened that email first.

> *Jean—*
> *I talked to Vicki at the SO—she manages the sheriff's calendar. She just laughed when I said we needed two or three days this week before the deposition. She can't manage more than an hour on Thursday at 2 pm or Friday after three. You'll have to talk to the sheriff personally to arrange something more. Vicki wouldn't give me the sheriff's cell but I gave her your number for the Sheriff to call you tonight. I hope that was okay.*

Jean sighed, unhappy but not surprised. She spared an ungracious thought for her boss, who should have had the sheriff scheduled for deposition preparation weeks ago. She could probably kiss her weekend goodbye, assuming that she could even get the sheriff to agree to meet her.

The elevator took her eight floors down. The main county administration building was the tallest in downtown Tesóro, giving her a nice view from her office of what skyline a city with a population of just under a hundred thousand people could offer. The town had been founded in the 1850s during the Pike's Peak Gold Rush, but most of the downtown dated from the steel mill boom of the early twentieth century. The existence of the mill and its strong history of labor unions led to the anomaly of a fairly liberal town in a largely conservative state.

It was too late to stop by the dry cleaners, so the only errand she had to run was dinner. The diner or takeout? She settled for chicken Caesar salad at a drive-through and ate it in her living room.

Charlotte would have been appalled. "For crissakes," she would have said. "Is it too much trouble to get some fresh romaine and cut up a chicken breast?"

Jean shook her head at the salad. She tossed the empty container into the recycling bin and checked her personal email account. She was reading an email from her friend Maryke in Dallas when her cell phone rang. She didn't know the number on the caller ID so she answered, "Jean McAllister."

"This is Sheriff Hawkins," a woman's brisk voice said. "Sorry for calling so late."

"No problem." Jean used her best professional tone. Her job depended to a certain extent on maintaining good relationships with the county elected officials. "I appreciate that you took the time to call."

"I understand you need some time on my schedule."

Jean launched into an explanation of the deposition and the discovery process but Hawkins said, "I've been deposed before, so I understand. What I *don't* understand is why the deadline is so short."

Her tone was matter-of-fact rather than challenging but Jean knew she had to come up with an explanation. The question was: how to explain without bad-mouthing Del Franklin?

"I just received the case today," she said truthfully. "I apologize for the urgency, but I spent several hours today reviewing the case and I think we'll need a day or two to get you ready for the deposition."

Hawkins said in an even tone, "That doesn't really answer my question."

Police officers, Jean thought in exasperation. She consciously relaxed her tense shoulders. "That's true," she admitted, "but that's all I know to tell you."

There was a brief pause. Then Hawkins said, "All right. The only way this is going to work is for us to meet on Saturday. We can have as much time as we need and if we need more there's always Sunday."

"Reminds me of a former boss of mine who used to tell us on Fridays that there were only two days left in the work week," Jean said lightly. She was making an effort to connect on a human level with the brisk, low voice on the other end of the phone.

"That's certainly true this week," Hawkins answered dryly. "Look, do we need to meet at your office or can we do this somewhere else?"

The question surprised her. "It doesn't matter. All I need is my laptop and a table to put about a half-a-dozen file folders on. Why?"

"Would you be willing to come out to my house? I really should be available here during the day. I've got an office at the house we can use, and I think I can manage lunch as well."

"I, well, of course." Kids at home, Jean assumed. "Just tell me where and when."

Before she went to bed, she decided to do a little checking up on Sheriff Lea Hawkins. She pulled up the San Carlos County Sheriff's website.

The home page had a photo of Sheriff Hawkins in her uniform. She looked straight into the camera without smiling, the very picture of serious and dependable law enforcement. Jean tried to guess her age from the small photo: early to mid forties, Jean finally decided, a little young to be sheriff. Hawkins wore her light brown hair just to the bottom of her ears, revealing tiny earrings. She had a strong, chiseled face. Her skin looked tan and something about her looked as if she had some Hispanic blood. Jean clicked on the sheriff's bio and read it thoughtfully.

Hawkins had virtually inherited the sheriff's office. Her grandfather and uncle had been San Carlos County sheriffs before her and she'd worked her way up through the ranks, serving in uniform, detention and the detective bureau before being elected to her first term six years ago.

She'd grown up in San Carlos County, graduated from Joya High School in the suburb west of Tesóro, but Jean was surprised to see that her college degree was from the John Jay College of Criminal Justice in New York City. Well, that must have been a bit of culture shock.

There was no mention of a family, so Jean wondered if she'd omitted the information or if Hawkins was just dedicated to her career. She'd find out on Saturday, she supposed.

CHAPTER TWO

Jean walked rapidly toward the board of county commissioners' conference room. She'd had all of two minutes' notice to appear at the study session, the informal gathering where the board heard reports and recommendations from staff or presentations from outside groups that didn't require a formal public hearing. Apparently Del had decided that the board needed an update on pending litigation and had called Rita to send down his new deputy. Jean was rapidly getting tired of always being at Franklin's beck and call. Maybe it was a power thing, she thought in irritation.

She arrived at the door to the conference room just as it opened. Stepping back quickly to avoid a collision, she looked up to see the woman she'd seen in the photo, Sheriff Hawkins, leaving.

"Sorry," Hawkins said briefly. She began to move away down the hall.

"Sheriff," Jean said quickly. "I'm Jean McAllister. We spoke on the phone last night."

Hawkins stopped and turned toward her. She was only a little taller than Jean, but her supple frame made her look even taller despite the bulk of the heavy duty belt she wore with her uniform. Jean keenly felt the extra ten pounds—okay, twelve pounds—she'd gained in the last year and a half. Sheriff Hawkins looked, as she had in her photo, to be the epitome of a law enforcement professional. There was a thin, faint scar that followed the line of her eyebrow above her left eye that Jean hadn't seen in the photograph.

Jean offered her hand and Hawkins took it, shaking it with a firm grip. "Nice to meet you in person, Counselor."

Jean decided she liked being called counselor. "Thanks again for taking the time to see me this weekend, Sheriff."

One side of Hawkins's mouth crooked upward. "We didn't have much choice, did we? In case I forgot to mention it, don't dress up. No need to wear the lawyer suit."

Jean glanced down at her conservative navy skirt and matching jacket. "Don't worry. I never wear pantyhose unless absolutely required."

Hawkins spared a brief glance at her legs and Jean felt a flare of curiosity. She'd always thought her legs were her best feature. Hawkins said, "Not wearing pantyhose is a good rule. It was my main reason for going into law enforcement. The avoidance of pantyhose, I mean."

Jean laughed. "Well, that's a fine rationale for a career choice."

Del Franklin appeared in the doorway behind them. "McAllister, what the hell are you...oh, Sheriff." His tone changed at once from annoyance to unctuous anxiety. "I didn't realize you were still here."

"Just meeting my new lawyer," Hawkins said coolly. "I need to get to another meeting. It was nice to meet you, Ms. McAllister. I'll see you on Saturday."

She left and Franklin muttered, "Enough chitchat. The board is waiting for us."

The three board members were seated at the conference room table. The windows on one side faced west to give them a fine view of the Rocky Mountains. They were still a month or more away from any snow so the mountaintops were a clear blue-gray against a cloudless afternoon sky.

Jean took a seat with her back to the view and concentrated on the board. The chair was Jaime Fontana, a heavy-set man with black hair he slicked back with too much Brylcreem. Apparently he'd never heard that he only needed a little dab. Jean remembered hearing that he always used his full name on his campaign posters. It emphasized that he was both Hispanic and Italian and linked him to both of the largest minorities in the county. He'd been on the board the longest, halfway through his third four-year term. It would be his last, as he was term-limited.

Next to Fontana was Hayward Lyons, the newest commissioner. He'd previously served as the county public works director, making the jump from employee to elected official two years ago. Jean couldn't imagine wanting to make the switch herself. Lyons was Ichabod Crane–thin with a prominent Adam's apple.

Del Franklin went around to sit next to Carolyn Forsythe. She was the commissioner representing the northern part of the county, which included the higher income suburbs of Tesóro. Jean knew little about Forsythe, but she looked like every well-dressed matron Jean had ever met: nice manicure, hair carefully held in place with hairspray, outfit completed with matching earrings and necklace. She wore sizable diamonds on both ring fingers.

Franklin refilled a water glass and set it on the coaster in front of Carolyn.

"Oh, thank you, Del." She all but patted his hand.

"Of course." He smiled broadly at her. "Let me know if you need anything else."

He smirked possessively. Yuck, Jean thought. She was never sure if her aversion to the more overt rituals of heterosexual mating was because she was gay or because they just reminded her of her mother, who was currently on husband number four. In this case, she decided, she just didn't want to watch her married boss flirting with one of his presumably married employers.

"You remember my new deputy attorney, Jean McAllister," Franklin said. There were nods from the men and a fluttery "Hello" from Carolyn Forsythe. "She's here to give you an update on our pending litigation cases."

He sat back and crossed his arms, apparently turning the meeting over to her. Thanks for the heads-up, Jean thought.

She ran through the minor cases first. There were a couple of land use appeals and a breach of contract case by a subcontractor. Jean gave the board members a couple of sentences apiece on where each case was in the court system. Then she started in on the major litigation, outlining several personal injury cases.

"You can update them on Lambert as well," Franklin said suddenly.

Jean blinked at him in annoyance. Franklin was handling that case, a federal court lawsuit involving a former public works employee who claimed he'd been wrongfully terminated by the county.

"Fred Lambert's a pain in the ass," Hayward Lyons said suddenly. "Road and bridge crews are always whining about something or other."

Fontana asked, "Are we talking about settlement? We could—"

"Waste of time," Lyons interrupted, his Adam's apple bobbing as he spoke. "Lambert's a liar who just wants to stir up trouble."

Jean cleared her throat, careful not to contradict him directly. "We'll have a mandatory settlement conference next month and we'll be coming to the board for settlement authority before that. I imagine we're looking at low six figures."

"Doesn't matter," Lyons muttered. "He won't take it. He wants to drag us into court."

Sounds personal, Jean thought. "We'll have a more in-depth analysis of our exposure for you when we talk about settlement authority. That leaves us with the Rosales case, the wrongful death suit by the family of the inmate who died while incarcerated in our jail."

Franklin interjected, "The board will recall that I discussed this lawsuit with you earlier this year. Since Ms. McAllister handled a number of similar cases in California, I thought this would be a good one to get her feet wet."

Seriously? Jean struggled not to let her emotions show. *You dumped this disorganized mess of a case in my lap a month before the discovery deadline for my own benefit? How thoughtful.*

"Is that wise?" Fontana demanded. "I mean, with all due respect to Ms. McAllister here, don't you think we should have our biggest gun on the case? They're suing us for a hell of a lot of money."

"Seven million dollars," Jean interjected smoothly.

Franklin's face darkened. "The case needs someone who can devote twenty-four seven to it if necessary and as you know, my other duties and responsibilities for the board are very time-consuming."

Carolyn Forsythe said, "Jaime, I'm sure Del knows what he's doing. Let's let him run his office, all right?"

Jean saw Fontana wince as Carolyn mispronounced his name, mangling the Spanish by pronouncing the first letter as *J* rather than *H*. Meanwhile, Del favored Carolyn with another smile.

Lyons said, "So what's our position? Did the sheriff fuck up?" He looked cheerful at the possibility.

"Now, Ward," Carolyn chided Lyons.

Jean wasn't sure if her disapproval extended to his language or his hostility to the sheriff. Jean answered, "The plaintiff is scheduled to depose the sheriff next week so I'll know more after that. My preliminary review of the case doesn't reveal any obvious breaches of procedure on the part of the sheriff's office. Mr. Rosales was in his cell when he began acting aggressively, yelling and pounding on the walls, when they sent in the extraction unit. He resisted and they attempted to restrain him. Eventually the extraction team used electroshock weapons but they were ineffective. They were forced to subdue him physically, then noticed he wasn't breathing. The medical unit was unable to revive him."

"Wait a minute," Fontana said. "I thought those stun gun things basically short-circuited your nervous system. How could they not work?"

Jean was grateful she'd had time to do some research on this point before this morning. "The shock weapon works most of the time but not always. If the subject is, for example, high on certain drugs, they may still be able to move even after the shock is applied."

"Was this guy Rosales on something?" Lyons asked.

She shook her head. "No, he'd been in the detention center for about twelve hours before the incident. But there's evidence he may have been suffering from a condition known as excited delirium. If he was, the weapons wouldn't have had an effect on him."

"So what killed him?" Fontana wanted to know.

Jean grimaced. "That's the problem. The death certificate gives the cause of death as 'respiratory arrest.' Excited delirium isn't a diagnosis accepted by everyone in the medical community, but if Rosales was suffering from it, it's likely what killed him. It causes cardiac or respiratory arrest."

Carolyn asked, "So how do you get this excited delirium?"

"It's usually a result of mental illness or drug abuse. The problem is that there's no way now to prove he was suffering from excited delirium and the plaintiff is, not surprisingly, claiming that it was the use of the stun guns that led to the respiratory arrest that killed him."

"So is that it?" Fontana asked. "We're fighting over this excited delirium thing?"

"Not exactly," Jean answered. She was dismayed that the board members had so little understanding of the liability issues for local government. Surely Franklin had told them all this before. "In order to recover," she continued, "the plaintiffs have to prove that the sheriff had a policy of deliberate indifference. In other words, it can't just be an accidental death; it has to be due to a defective policy or procedure on the part of the detention center."

"Well?" Lyons demanded, his Adam's apple bobbing again. "Can they prove that?"

Fontana said, "Come on, Ward. You know Lea. Nobody runs a tighter ship. We should be good to go."

He looked confidently at Jean, who said, "I'll know more after the deposition next week, but I'm hopeful we'll either be able to get the court to dismiss the case on a Motion for Summary Judgment, or at least arrange for a very reasonable settlement."

Franklin shuffled papers together, muttering, "All right, we need to move on. McAllister, send in the water board director, will you? He should be right outside."

Aye, aye, Captain. Jean bristled at his summary dismissal, but picked up her legal pad. She said her goodbyes to the board members. Carolyn ignored her, seemingly engrossed in something Franklin was saying softly to her.

Jean escaped to her office and the pile of work sprawled across her desk.

CHAPTER THREE

The City of Tesóro was divided into quarters by the two highways that crossed it. Interstate 25 ran approximately north-south, roughly paralleling the line of the Rocky Mountains from Wyoming on down into New Mexico, like a backbone through the state of Colorado. Highway 54 was the main east-west thoroughfare, winding into the mountains west of town and extending across the southeastern plains to the east. Tesóro's downtown centered on the intersection of the two highways, the working class neighborhoods with their tiny frame houses at the southern end of the city. To the west lay the unincorporated settlement of Joya where the houses were built on one- or two-acre lots, many with either horse barns or giant garages for recreational vehicles and boats. Beyond that, tucked against the foothills, were a few larger holdings, left over from the huge cattle ranches of the 1800s. Jean had looked up the name "Joya" online—it meant "jewel," which made sense since the name of the city, Tesóro, meant "treasure."

The directions Jean received from Sheriff Hawkins were taking her west to the boundaries of Joya. She turned north off Highway 54 onto a county road until she saw the sign for Painted Horse Ranch. She turned onto the road and a couple of miles later she saw the ranch house.

She maneuvered her sedan down the long graveled driveway. The house was set on a little rise, facing west. As Jean got out of her car, wrestling with briefcase and laptop, she spared a moment to admire the view. There were clouds this morning, fluffy white with flat gray bottoms, hanging as if suspended over the blue peaks of the mountains.

Jean walked up the driveway with the gravel crunching under her feet.

Unlike many of the homes in Joya, which favored an adobe look, this was a typical ranch house, a single story with a friendly-looking wraparound front porch. It would have been perfectly at home on the Ponderosa.

Sheriff Hawkins was waiting for her, comfortably seated in a rocker on the porch, cowboy boots propped on the railing. Hawkins was wearing dark wash blue jeans and a light blue denim western-style shirt. She looked completely at home, as if she could leap onto a bucking bronco at any moment.

On the table beside her lay her cell phone and a thick white mug with steam gently rising.

"Good morning, Sheriff," Jean greeted her. She is really a handsome woman, Jean thought suddenly. Strong features and intelligent eyes.

"Good morning to you, Counselor," Hawkins responded. "Why don't you put that stuff down for a couple of minutes and let me get you a cup of coffee? It's too nice a morning to rush inside."

Jean gratefully dumped her burden onto the table. She smiled and said, "Coffee would be great, thanks."

"Sugar? Half-and-half?"

"Just black."

She settled into the second rocking chair and when Hawkins brought her a mug, she sipped happily. "This is really good, thanks."

Hawkins resumed her seat. "All ranchers can make good coffee and good steaks. Anything else is a bonus."

Jean laughed. "What about beans?"

"I forgot about beans. But in all fairness, it's hard to screw up beans."

"Good point." Jean relaxed into the morning air, still with a faint scent of sage and cool breeze. The high desert would warm quickly but in this moment the temperature seemed perfect.

To her surprise, Hawkins didn't say anything for a while and Jean felt herself relax even more. Everything here in San Carlos moved more slowly than she was accustomed to and she was constantly slowing herself down to meet the pace. The coffee was rich and the view of blue mountains and sandy ground, studded with dark green vegetation, soothed her.

At length she said, "So are you really a rancher at heart, Sheriff?"

Hawkins seemed to consider the question seriously. That bodes well for her deposition testimony, Jean thought.

Hawkins answered, "Not really. Law enforcement is what I'm about. But my mother's family has owned this land for almost two hundred years and ran cattle on it until just a few years ago. So I come from a long line of ranchers. My grandfather and my father's younger brother were San Carlos sheriffs before I was." She threw a sidelong glance at Jean and added, "But I imagine you knew that already."

"You assumed I checked you out before showing up today?" Jean's tone was tart.

"Yep. And just so you know, I did the same. I wanted to know about my new lawyer."

Jean hadn't thought of that. "So did you approve of what you found out?"

Hawkins drank coffee. "Undergrad and law school at the University of Texas, six years private practice in California, eleven years in the Riverside County attorney's office defending lawsuits against various county officials. Those ought to be qualifications enough."

"Glad I have your approval, Sheriff," Jean said sharply.

Hawkins responded mildly, "You've got a big case landed in your lap with virtually no time to prepare and my office's reputation is at stake. Of course I checked you out. Everyone told me you're a good lawyer and a fine litigator. So let's get to work. And by the way, save the sheriff stuff for the courtroom. My friends call me Lea." She pronounced it like "Lee" instead of the two-syllable "Le-ah" Jean might have assumed.

She rose and helped Jean pick up the file folders.

They walked through the living room and Jean exclaimed, "What a gorgeous fireplace!"

Massive stones in the colors of the landscape outside, chocolate and mocha, framed the hearth from ceiling to floor. A huge pine mantel supported an assortment of objects: candlesticks, a stack of books, a few photographs in wooden frames, a hunting knife in a sheath, a box of wooden matches, a pottery vase with a few branches of sage, an old battered clock. The room was fairly tidy, although a stack of magazines was stacked haphazardly on the coffee table and a book was open on the arm of an armchair.

"Thanks," Lea said. "I spent most of the money for the house on it. Well, that and the kitchen. And the bathtub."

"You built the house?" Jean asked. The building looked so old-fashioned she'd just assumed it was many years old.

"Yep. I wanted to live close to my family without living with them, so my parents deeded me a few acres and I've been here ever since."

First person singular, Jean mused. Did she live here alone? Aloud she said, "Bathtub?"

Lea laughed, a deep rich sound. "I always wanted one of those big claw-foot tubs and I got one. They cost a fortune, but there's nothing like hot bathwater up to your chin after a long day in meetings."

Jean cleared her throat to dispel the image. She murmured, "Sounds nice."

The first bedroom in the hall had been turned into Lea's office and Lea insisted that Jean take the office chair. "Set up your laptop if you want and I'll sit here in the witness chair."

When Jean was ready, she said, "I know you said you've been deposed before, but I'd like to remind you of a few things. The purpose of the deposition is discovery, for the other side to find out about the facts of our case. It's supposed to prevent surprise at trial and how the discovery goes helps set the stage for settlement discussions as well as motions that might get us out of the suit early."

Lea seemed to be following her, so Jean continued, "The problem is that I don't know the attorneys on the other side so I can't guess how competent they are. If they're not experienced or just not very good, things could go south."

"How so?" Lea asked.

Jean sighed. "Plaintiffs' attorneys especially have a tendency to argue with witnesses as if they could somehow compel you to agree with them if they just harass you enough. They might try to confuse you, badger you or deliberately misinterpret what you say. There's no judge or jury in the room so there's no one to curb some pretty unsavory practices."

Lea lifted one corner of her mouth. "Except you, my hard-working lawyer, of course."

"Except me," Jean agreed. "I can make an objection for the record but you'll have to answer unless they really get inappropriate. If I instruct you not to answer, then don't. But the truth is that discovery isn't just to establish admissible evidence. The rules of procedure say that anything that might *lead* to admissible evidence is the subject of discovery and that's pretty broad. So they can go a long way with their questioning and there's only so much I can do. But there's a lot *you* can do."

Lea leaned forward, her eyes bright and sharp. "Well by all means, tell me."

"Don't answer a question unless you understand it," Jean began. "All you have to say is 'I don't understand' and they'll have to rephrase it until you do. Don't try to answer a question if you're not sure of the answer. It's perfectly fine to say 'I don't know.' I know there's a lot of pressure when you're being questioned and you can get into a rhythm of trying to answer everything, but the fastest way to get into trouble is to try to come up with an answer when you're not sure. Sometimes they try to confuse things by asking you the same question several times. I can object, but you can control that more easily by just saying, 'I've already answered the question.' They hate that."

"It's a little like an interview during an investigation," Lea said.

"Is it?"

"It can be like a game," Lea explained patiently. "The witness or the suspect has something you want and sometimes they're willing to give it to you and sometimes they're not and sometimes they don't even know what you want. So you have to figure out how to get it."

"Fair enough," Jean agreed. "What we're going to do is this: I'm going to harass the hell out of you today so by the time they get to ask you the same questions next week, you'll already know where to go with the answers. I'll show you the documents they'll probably ask you to explain and try to think of every possible question they could come up with. Okay?"

"Will you actually ask me any questions at the deposition itself?"

"Probably a few, but only to clarify something you said. I don't have to use the deposition to get information from you. I can get that anytime."

Lea gave her the crooked smile again. "You've got my number."

Jean pulled up her list of sample questions on her laptop screen. "They'll go over your background, training, experience, things like that first, so we'll start there. But before we begin, I have to ask you something awkward. Is there anything they could ask you that would be embarrassing or difficult to explain?"

The smile vanished and Lea leaned back, one finger tapping on the arm of her chair.

"Like what?" Her voice was cooler.

"Anything. Complaints filed against you for excessive force or allegations of misuse of funds?"

Lea uncrossed her legs, crossed them again and shifted in her chair. Jean was beginning to suspect that Lea had something she didn't want to discuss.

Finally Lea shook her head. "Nothing like that."

Jean sighed. "Or it could be something personal."

"Personal?" Lea's voice was low and sharp.

Jean nodded. "Could be anything. A DUI. A nasty divorce. I once had a lawyer try to embarrass a social worker when I was defending the department of human services by bringing up the fact that she was living with her boyfriend 'outside the bonds of matrimony.'"

"You're kidding."

"No. The lawyer was a creep but it did rattle my witness for a while. The best way to handle something like that is to know about the possibility ahead of time and be honest about it."

Lea was frowning now. "How could something personal like that possibly be relevant to the case?"

"It's not," Jean said, "but as I told you, the rules of civil procedure are so broad, they can bring up all kinds of shit in discovery. And they will."

Lea was silent for a long time. She had grown still, her only movement the quietly tapping forefinger. Jean looked down at Lea's hands: they looked strong. They were working hands, like those of a chef or a pianist, with long tapering fingers.

"I don't know you," Lea said at length.

The comment startled Jean. "What?"

"I don't really know anything about you. Other people say you're a good lawyer, but why would I trust you with something personal?"

Jean was faintly shocked. "I'm your attorney."

The half smile returned. "Forgive me, but that doesn't necessarily mean I can trust you."

Lea seemed genuinely worried so Jean said lightly, "What? Are you saying all attorneys aren't worthy of your utmost faith?"

Lea caught the tone. She said, "Okay, all right, I get it. It's just…"

Her voice trailed off and Jean got a sudden insight. Was she just indulging in wishful thinking? The possibility jolted her a little, but she knew a quick way to resolve the situation.

Jean said abruptly, "I'm a lesbian."

A lock of wavy hair fell over Lea's forehead. "What?"

"You heard me."

Lea was staring at her and for a moment Jean feared that she'd been wrong. Men and women in law enforcement tended to be more conservative than otherwise. Was Sheriff Hawkins a homophobe? *Hell, I've stepped in it now.* Jean braced for her reaction.

"Why would you tell me that?" Lea asked finally.

"Now that I've told you something personal," Jean explained, "maybe you can feel better about whatever it is you need to tell me." She crossed her fingers under the desk, hoping fervently that whatever it was, it wasn't going to be a major issue.

Lea looked out the window at the view of the desert visible through the glass and Jean followed her gaze. Sandy soil supported a surprising variety of small trees, piñon and mesquite, few of which grew taller than six feet. At length Lea said, "So you're not just pulling my chain or something?"

"Of course not," Jean said quickly. "I'm telling you the truth, believe me. I wouldn't joke about that."

Lea sighed deeply and Jean could see in her expression that she had come to a final conclusion. "Here's the thing," Lea began. "It's not really a secret. My family knows, a few people in my office know, a couple of people in the county are aware as well. I've never lied about it, it just doesn't come up. It's like a weird 'don't ask, don't tell' deal I have with the county voters. I don't really talk about it and no one has ever asked me about it."

Jean said, "Um, what are we talking about, exactly?"

"Oh, sorry," Lea said. "I thought you'd figured it out. Me too. I mean, I'm gay."

Jean blew out the breath she'd been holding and uncrossed her fingers. *Thank you, God.*

"Okay," she said briskly as she rearranged her paperwork. "Chances are it won't come up at all and if it does, I'll certainly object on the grounds of relevance. But if you're compelled to answer, tell the truth. Always tell the truth."

The half-grin reappeared. "What kind of lawyer are you, Ms. McAllister? Advising your clients to tell the truth like that."

"Very funny. Now that we've got all of this settled, it's Jean, all right?"

"All right. And since you didn't ask, I'm not in a relationship now and haven't been for a couple of years."

I wonder what the ex was like. The thought came unbidden to Jean and she shook her head to be rid of it. "Got it. Anything else you need to tell me?"

Lea said dryly, "Sometimes I forget to recycle and just throw my cans and bottles into the regular trash."

"Oh, my God!" Jean exclaimed in mock horror. "Well, if they find out, we're going to have to settle the case right away. How awful."

The moment relaxed them and Lea eased back into her chair. "Okay, Counselor. Bring it on."

* * *

Two hours later Jean took off her glasses and rubbed the bridge of her nose. "I don't know about you but I could use a break."

Lea stretched out her legs. She said, "Absolutely. Let me just say I'm glad you're on my side because I wouldn't want you asking those questions for real."

"You've done really well," Jean said. "We went much faster than I thought we would. If you can stay that cool during the real deposition, we'll be in fine shape."

Lea did have a calm, almost zenlike quality about her that Jean admired. It probably came in very handy in emergencies.

Lea stood and lifted her arms overhead, moving slowly side to side to realign her spine. On her right hip, Jean glimpsed a small gun holstered at her waistband. Lea caught her gaze. She asked quietly, "Does that make you uncomfortable?"

The question surprised Jean. "No. I guess I'm just a little stunned that you're wearing a weapon in your own home."

"I'm always armed," Lea said gravely, "unless I'm asleep. I'm the chief law enforcement officer for San Carlos County and I'm accountable for the safety of every citizen here. I take that responsibility seriously."

Jean smiled, hoping she hadn't offended her new client. "As a new citizen of San Carlos County," she said easily, "I thank you. And now, I think I'd like to visit the nearest bathroom."

"Second door on your right in the hallway. I need to make a brief phone call and then we can talk about a very late lunch."

"Sounds great."

As Jean washed her hands, she glanced around the bathroom. Black iron horseshoes screwed into the wall held the guest towels and an attractive turquoise wall highlighted the room. But like all rooms designed for guests, it was impersonal and told her nothing about the owner.

Jean was the first to admit that she had a serious problem with, well, snooping. She could call it curiosity and it was in a way, but it was mostly just nosiness. She had often pried into her mother's dresser drawers when she was young and she still had a strong urge to check out other people's kitchen cabinets. She tried to convince herself that it was this quality that made her a good legal researcher.

She stepped into the hallway and heard Lea still talking on the telephone in the kitchen, so she wandered down the hall. The room next door was actually a gym, weight bench and free weights neatly aligned. A treadmill was set up to take advantage of the eastern view at the back of the house. Nice for morning runs, Jean thought. She went across the hall, still reassured by Lea's voice in the kitchen and peeked into the master bedroom.

Like the living room, the room was tidy without being perfect. A couple of books were stacked on the nearest nightstand next to what looked like a good reading lamp. The alarm clock, with its iPhone jack empty, was on the same side. A padded rocking chair took up one corner and a sweatshirt was draped over one arm.

Lea's voice rose with the sounds of saying goodbye, so Jean retreated down the hall and arrived in the kitchen as Lea said, "Okay. Call me if you need anything before Dad gets home. Love you."

She punched the phone off. Jean asked, "Everything all right?"

Lea looked at her with a moment of evaluation before answering, "Yes. My father is gone for the day delivering a horse to a customer and my mother is home alone with my brother. I needed to be here in case they needed anything."

Jean's first thought was, wonder what's wrong with the brother? As if Lea had read her thought, she continued, "My brother is in a wheelchair. He's pretty independent, but my mother can't lift him if there's a problem so I wanted to be close by."

She moved to the counter and got out flour tortillas, reaching into the refrigerator for shredded cheese and salsa. "I thought quesadillas, will that work?"

"Sounds fine. May I help?"

"Nope, it'll just take a couple of minutes. Why don't you just sit at the counter and we'll eat in here."

Lea assembled the meal. Jean watched her hands, graceful despite their strength. After a minute Jean asked, "Your father raises horses?"

"Yes. After my parents decided running cattle didn't make economic sense, he decided to breed paint horses. He always liked horses better than cows anyway." She gave the half smile that Jean was beginning to realize was characteristic. "He always says that cows are the dumbest creatures God ever made, other than men."

Jean expected her to use the microwave but Lea plucked an iron skillet from the rack above her head and griddled the quesadillas until the cheese was hot and gooey.

Jean ate with her usual enthusiasm and Lea seemed to regard her with amusement.

"This salsa is great," Jean muttered through her tortilla. "Did you make it yourself?"

"Well, it's my mother's recipe but I did chop the onions," Lea responded. "She always makes sure she has assistants around when it's time to chop something."

Jean smiled. "Can't have too many sous-chefs."

"Excuse me?"

Jean winced. "Sorry. That's fancy French for assistant cook in charge of chopping." She changed the subject. "So your mother is the family chef?"

"Yep. She has mastered the art of traditional Mexican dishes, New Mexican, Tex-Mex and cooking any cut of beef you can name. She also makes a mean hollandaise sauce."

"Hollandaise? Hardly a traditional south-of-the-border sauce."

"It's for a southwestern eggs benedict my mother makes that you'll have to try sometime. Better than huevos rancheros by a long shot."

"Sounds great," Jean said, finishing her quesadilla. Was she being invited to a future brunch at the Hawkins's ranch? She found she liked the idea.

"You're close to your family," she said as Lea began to collect the empty dishes.

"Old-fashioned though it may sound," Lea said, "I believe in family and home and community. It's easy for me because I have a great family and a wonderful place to live." She looked out the window over the sink a moment and added, "I truly can't imagine living anywhere else."

Jean interjected, "Not even New York?"

Lea turned toward her, shaking her head. "Spending four years in New York was very important. How can you know where you should be if you've never tried anywhere else? New York City is a giant of a place, the greatest big city in the world. But it's still a city and I knew I wouldn't be happy there. As soon as I got back here, I could breathe again. I knew where I belonged. I've never regretted it."

What would that feel like to know where your home really is? Jean sat quietly and wondered. Texas was where she was from, but neither her mother's houses nor her boarding school had ever felt like home. She'd chosen southern California herself and after she met Charlotte, Palm Springs had been home—hadn't it? Not really, she acknowledged. Palm Springs was lovely in the winter, but Charlotte had been home for her. She would have gone anywhere with Char, at least in the beginning of the relationship. Then later there was nowhere to go, nowhere that mattered.

They were finished by five o'clock, faster than Jean could have hoped for. It had taken them a long time to go over the coroner's report. Jean reminded Lea more than once not to guess or speculate on facts she couldn't know. Once Lea got the concept she was rock solid and Jean felt satisfied that she'd covered everything she needed.

She was packing up when Lea's cell phone rang. "Go ahead," she reassured Lea.

"Hi, Mom, how's it going?" After a moment, Lea said sharply, "What happened? Is he all right?"

Jean felt herself tense up. What was worse, bad news by telephone or in person? She'd had plenty of experience with both and could never decide.

After Lea listened intently for a moment, she said, "Okay. I'm on my way. No, it's fine, we're done here."

She punched the phone off. She asked, "Can you get back out to the highway? I need to go to the house."

"Of course. Is everything okay?"

"I think so. My dad had a flat tire so he'll be late getting back and my brother fell in the barn. He says he's okay, but I need to go make sure."

Jean, her arms full of briefcase and file folders, hesitated for a moment, then said, "Do you want me to go with you? Maybe I can help."

Lea gave her an appraising look. "You don't need to do that."

"I'm sure you can handle it," Jean added hastily, "but you might need another pair of hands."

Lea seemed to be evaluating her, as if trying to decide whether the offer was perfunctory or sincere. "All right," she said at last. "If you're sure, follow me over and then you can leave in your own car whenever you want."

Jean wasn't sure why she offered to go. Despite how tired she was after the day of work, for some reason going back to her condo alone had suddenly lost its appeal.

CHAPTER FOUR

The Hawkins family house was a couple of miles away, a beautiful hacienda-style home with whitewashed walls. In front of the long one-story building, native flowers and grasses had been carefully planted and maintained to create a high desert garden: purple salvia, red, orange and yellow Indian paintbrush and many others Jean didn't know. White columns supported a saltillo tile roof, which provided shade for a porch that ran the length of the entire front of the house. The red-orange roof tiles made it seem to Jean as if the sun would appear to be always setting over the rooftop. Benches and rocking chairs along the covered porch, many with horse blanket-style cushions, were proof that the porch was well used by family members.

As Jean got out of her car, a pair of big dogs rounded the house in a headlong rush straight for Lea. Jean stood still, wary but not afraid, as the two circled Lea. Both dogs were madly barking and romping happily.

Lea looked over at Jean and grinned. "The family guard dogs. They're very fierce, as you can see."

A moment later the dogs were attacking Lea with wagging tails and frantic demands for petting. Jean laughed and asked, "Safe to approach?"

"Yes, if you don't mind being licked half to death."

Jean came forward and gave each dog a good sniff of her hand. Tail wagging resumed, but before they could exercise bad manners and jump on her, Lea said sternly, "Wyatt, Doc. Sit. Stay."

Both dogs obediently if reluctantly went down on their haunches and Jean leaned over to reward them with ear-rubbing.

"Which is which?" she asked.

"Wyatt is the black and white, a mix of our neighbor's border collie and we think a wandering black lab. Doc Holliday, who despite the name is female, is a German shepherd mix we got from the shelter. They're both mongrels but good dogs."

"We're all mongrels, aren't we?" Jean said absently.

Lea smiled crookedly. "Yep, we are at that. Come on, the barn's this way."

They went around the house with the dogs trailing happily behind them, bouncing like canine rubber balls. The barn was huge. It was another classic building, painted red and immaculate. The crisp scent of fresh hay and the warm smell of horse filled her nostrils as Jean entered. Halfway down the center aisle a man in a wheelchair sat talking with a woman. He looked up and she heard him say, "Cavalry's here, Ma."

The woman turned and came toward them. She had a face that hinted of her Mexican heritage. Her dark brown hair was almost black except where it was threaded with gray. Her smooth olive skin betrayed only a few lines around her mouth and eyes. Jean could see Lea's cheekbones and jaw in her face. Jean tried to guess her age, which could have been anywhere north of sixty based on her appearance.

The woman said briskly, "I swear he's more stubborn than your father and that's saying a lot."

"What's going on?" Lea asked calmly.

"He fell and he won't let me check him for injuries, the bull-headed—"

The man interrupted her by calling out, "I can hear you, Ma, and I'm way past the age where I need my mother to pull my jeans down!"

"I see he got back up into the chair all right," Lea said.

"Oh yes, he's strong enough, he just makes your average mule look tractable." She turned to Jean. "I'm sorry to meet you in the midst of a minor family crisis. I'm Linda Hawkins. Welcome to the Painted Horse Ranch." Jean could hear the pride in her voice.

Jean offered her hand. "Jean McAllister. I'm the deputy county attorney."

Lea added, "She's my new lawyer."

"Well, thank heavens for that." Linda gave Jean a friendly chuckle. "I never met a woman who needed a lawyer more." Linda turned to Lea and said, "Will you go talk some reason to your brother before I go out back and cut a switch to paddle him with?"

The man called again, "That threat won't work. I can't feel it!"

Linda Hawkins rolled her eyes as Lea went over to him. Jean tried hard not to laugh aloud.

"That stubborn excuse for a cowboy is my son Loren," Linda said. "He apparently takes being in a wheelchair as a challenge to see just how banged up he can get. Lea's the only one who can talk any sense to him. He and his father just end up shouting, though I suspect it's therapeutic for both of them."

Over by her brother, Lea burst out laughing and gestured for Jean and her mother to join them. When they arrived, Jean looked down to see a handsome man, perhaps in his late thirties, wearing a plaid western shirt, well-worn jeans and cowboy boots. He looked up with bright button brown eyes. "Very pleased to meet you. Lea says you're dynamite."

Does she? Jean thought. When did she have a chance to do that? "I'm happy to meet you too. Your mother says you give mules a run for their money in the stubbornness department."

"I've just thought of a compromise," Loren said with a wicked grin directed to Jean. "How about I let *you* conduct the examination? All you have to do is carefully inspect my naked behind to make sure I didn't bruise my delicate babylike bottom."

"Loren!" Linda chastised him.

Lea began laughing again. Jean considered her response for a moment. Lea had told her she was out to her family and they all seemed to be on good terms. Would they still react positively to Jean? "I would volunteer to check you out," Jean said as she made her decision, "but looking at a man's backside just wouldn't do a thing for me. Sorry."

Loren blinked in comprehension, then said, "Oh, crap. I finally meet a gorgeous new woman and she's on the other side of the fence. Lea, that's just cruel. So is she, at long last, the new girlfriend?"

It was Jean's turn to blink but Linda said, "This is Jean, Lea's new lawyer, so I expect you to behave yourself. She's not an option for the inspection so it's either your sister or me. Which will it be?"

He gave her a mock pout. "Sure I can't talk Jean into it? It may not be her idea of a rodeo, but I'd still prefer it. Or we could just wait till Dad gets home."

Linda was already shaking her head. "He won't be home for two or three hours yet and you know it's not safe to wait that long. You could be hurt and not know it."

Lea said pleasantly, "Come on, cowboy, let's get it over with." She glanced at Jean and added, "You're off duty. Thanks for the help and for harassing my brother. We get so few chances for it."

"Very funny," Loren said. "Give up being the sheriff and try for a career as a rodeo clown, why don't you?"

Linda said, "Don't be silly, Lea. Jean drove all the way out here, the least we can do is give her dinner."

"You don't need to do that," Jean demurred. "Lea fed me lunch."

"Lunch!" Linda huffed. "Let me guess. You got a quesadilla, right? That's not lunch, that's an appetizer. I insist that you stay for dinner. Lou won't be home until late and I have enough food for a roundup."

Jean found herself hustled into the house by Linda who led the way and the dogs who herded her from behind. Once inside the giant kitchen, complete with six-burner gas stove, double ovens and a huge island, Linda put her to work, chopping onions and peppers.

The two dogs circled the women in the kitchen trolling for tidbits. When none appeared, they meandered to a pair of dog beds in a corner of the living room. They lay down but remained alert for any food that might hit the floor.

Jean looked down at the neat piles of vegetables she'd created and wondered how long it had been since she'd plied a knife for *mise en place*.

At least one year, eight months and nine days.

Linda said approvingly, "You've done that before."

"I lived with a chef for thirteen years," Jean admitted. "She taught me a few things." She still felt tentative talking about her personal life with the sheriff's mother.

Linda scooped up the onions and chiles to dump them into a frying pan. With her back turned to Jean, she said casually, "So, a long-term relationship. Lea managed almost ten years. I'm so sick to death of people telling me about homosexuals and 'family values.' Harlan, who owns the nursery I use, has been with the same man for thirty years, give or take. Every gay person I know is or has been with the same partner for a long time, which is far from what I can say about many heterosexuals I know. Our neighbor but one to the south is married to his third wife, for heaven's sake."

Jean cleared her throat. "My mother is on husband number four."

"Oh, dear," Linda said sympathetically. "That must have been hard on you."

"It got easier when she sent me to boarding school when I was nine."

"So young! I couldn't imagine sending my children away."

"I was fine, actually. My mother was miserable when she was between men, which wasn't often and she drank too much when she was married. She still does."

"You're in touch with her?"

"Sort of. Not much," Jean admitted. "When I told her I was gay, she stopped talking to me. No scene, no screaming, just—nothing. I call on her birthday and at Christmas and we exchange about ten words. I do speak to my stepfather about once a month to check up on her. He's a nice guy, he's just co-dependent about her drinking."

"No siblings?" Linda asked.

"A younger brother. His preacher has informed him that I'm headed straight for hell so he stays far, far away from me to avoid any possible contamination."

Linda snorted in disapproval. Jean heard the bitterness in her own voice and became aware, as she often did these days, of how cold she was, even in the warm kitchen. Her hands felt icy and she suppressed a shiver.

Why was she telling Linda Hawkins her life story? It's been too long, she thought, since I talked to anyone about anything other than work. Moving from Southern California had been a good idea, but she had to find a gym or a book club or something, or she'd start collecting cats to have someone to have a conversation with, or begin chatting randomly to people on the street.

But Linda was easy to talk to and they spoke about recipes until Lea came in and went to the sink to wash her hands.

"How's Loren?" Linda asked.

"Fine. No injuries I can see. Dad should probably check him again tonight before bed to make sure there aren't bruises I didn't see yet. Loren said he just leaned out too far and fell on his butt. He's been hurt worse."

Linda smiled sadly. "I keep reminding myself the accident might have been a blessing in disguise. At least he's not risking his neck every week anymore."

Jean looked up curiously and Lea said, "Can I borrow the assistant for a minute?"

"Of course," Linda said. "Dinner is about half an hour off."

Lea took Jean back to her parents' office. Like everything else in the house it was about twice the size of a normal room.

The office was crowded with a large table next to a desk with a giant desktop computer surrounded by piles of messy paperwork. There was a second, smaller desk that held only a neatly centered laptop.

Lea gestured. "Dad's desk and Mom's desk. Bet you can guess which is which."

"Not too tough. Your mother has the cleanest non-commercial kitchen I've seen in a long time."

Lea led her to the pictures that covered the three non-windowed walls of the office. "One wall per child," she announced.

On the paneling to her right were pictures of a strongly built man with sandy hair. In the largest one he was wearing a Joya High School football uniform and next to the photo were a couple of framed newspaper articles and a certificate indicating that Lawrence Hawkins was a Colorado second-team all-state wide receiver. The next photo portrayed him in a Southeastern Colorado State uniform as he caught a football. Then the photographs changed, showing a man in an army uniform, along with pictures of his family: a pretty woman with two blond children, a boy and a girl.

"Is he still in the army?" Jean wanted to know.

"Second tour in the Middle East," Lea answered softly.

"How old are your niece and nephew now?"

"John is thirteen and Megan is eleven."

"Your brother decided not to continue the family tradition of giving everyone a name beginning with L?" Jean joked.

Lea laughed easily. "Mom always said it would make inheriting all the monogrammed towels and china easier later."

"Your mother has monogrammed towels and china?" Jean asked in surprise.

"Oh, hell no!" Lea laughed harder. "My mother is the least pretentious person I've ever met. She's also one of the smartest and certainly the kindest."

"You got lucky in the parent lottery, then," Jean said, wondering if she sounded bitter again.

"I did," Lea acknowledged. "But I think I should admit I don't actually have a name beginning with L."

Jean blinked. "So Lea is short for what?"

Lea sighed. "I was named after my grandmother. Rosalea Dolores Sanchez-Ortiz."

"Rosalea. Sounds very exotic."

Lea grinned. "A word no one would ever use to describe me. Come on, I mainly brought you in here to show you Loren's wall."

They crossed the room and Jean glanced at the photos of Loren the boy displayed on the wood paneling. In every photo Loren was in full western gear. Her favorite was a snapshot of the boy about eight or nine years old twirling a lasso while wearing a hat two sizes too big for his head. But most impressive were the shadow boxes with huge belt buckles mounted for display, shiny silver and gold with elaborate engravings. Some had pictures of bull riders, others had words like "Champion" or "Rodeo" engraved on them. Several were too huge to wear as actual belt buckles, fully six or seven inches across. Men and their obsession with size, Jean smiled to herself. Bigger was always better.

There were more photos to see: Loren on the back of a huge bull, one hand flung into the air as the animal plunged forward or Loren accepting one of the buckles at a rodeo. Lea pointed out the largest picture, Loren clamped on the back of a giant black bull as it twisted, all four hooves suspended above the dirt of the arena.

"That was his last ride," Lea said, soft pride and sadness mingling in her voice. "He won the championship at Cheyenne Frontier Days. The bull's name was 'Whiskey Cures Ugly.' It was a great ride."

"What happened? Was he thrown, or—"

Shaking her head, Lea said, "No. He was driving back from Cheyenne. He should have stayed overnight. He was too tired to drive safely but he wanted to get home. Fell asleep at the wheel. The pickup turned over and he broke his back."

"Oh, God. Poor guy. How long ago?"

"About four years now. The first year and a half or so were awful. It seemed like Loren lost everything. His wife cut out on him, he couldn't ride bulls anymore. He didn't want to live. He went through hell and my parents went through it with him every day."

"You too" Jean guessed quietly.

"All of us. If there's something worse than seeing someone you love suffering when you can't do anything to help, I don't know what it is."

Tears blurred her vision before Jean even knew they were there. What in the hell is wrong with me? She brushed them away quickly, but not before Lea said, "I'm sorry. I didn't mean to upset you."

"It's fine," Jean said brusquely. "It's just a sad story. I'm glad he's doing so much better. Don't you think I should get to see your trophies?"

Lea shrugged. "Nothing much to see."

"Oh, I doubt that," Jean said. She marched herself over to the third wall.

Childhood photographs showed a gangly Lea, usually on horseback. A couple of pictures displayed her as a teenager in a basketball uniform, bringing the ball up the court with a look of fierce concentration. Her certificate read First Team All-State Girl's Basketball.

"Gee, your brother only made second team in football," Jean said, joking to try to regain her composure.

"And I never let Larry forget it, believe me," Lea said, her half grin returning. "It's the duty of middle sisters to harass older brothers and torment younger brothers."

There were photos of Lea in her sheriff's uniform with hash marks increasing on her sleeves as she got older. Then a tiny gold medal appeared above her left breast and Jean stooped to read the citation framed next to the photograph that read "For Conspicuous Bravery in the Line of Duty."

"That sounds impressive," Jean commented. She wondered if it had something to do with the scar above Lea's eyebrow.

"Not much," Lea said casually. "Sheriffs offices and police departments are like the military. They love to give out fancy ribbons and geegaws."

"Geegaws? You actually use words like that in everyday conversation?"

"I pride myself on my colorful vocabulary."

Jean finished scanning Lea's wall. It was filled with certificates of appreciation from various law enforcement agencies or letters of praise from the distinguished. Lea said, "This is pretty boring but it makes my parents happy to look at all this stuff. Come on, dinner's got to be ready by now."

They carried thick terra-cotta bowls to the table with a platter piled with homemade flour tortillas. After the first bite of chili, Jean looked at Linda in shock.

"It's a little hot," Linda said calmly, "but you'll get used to it. Loren was eating it when he was three."

Loren was shoveling in the spicy chili but managed to grin. "Ma, I swear I get younger every time you tell that story."

Jean groped for her water glass, but Lea said, "Water won't help. Eat some tortilla. The starch will help cut the heat."

Giving her a skeptical look, Jean tore off a triangle of tortilla and chewed vigorously. After a couple of minutes, the fire in her mouth seemed to ease.

"Sure you don't want a beer?" Loren asked, taking another healthy swig from his own bottle.

Jean shook her head. After so many years of smelling alcohol on her mother's breath and having the scent of it on her clothes, drinking had never appealed to her. She noticed that Lea wasn't drinking either and wondered about it. Linda was sipping Dos Equis from a glass while Loren took his beer straight from the bottle.

Jean managed to polish off about half her chili and helped Linda take the bowls in to the kitchen. "Grab the plates, will you?" Linda asked.

She scooped chicken smothered in onions and peppers onto the plates and Jean realized she would need to pace herself to get through the food. Apparently the chili was only the first course.

The dinner conversation covered a wide variety of topics from horses to the history of the ranch to Jean's travels. After a while, Loren asked his sister, "You making any progress on the burglaries?"

Lea shook her head. "No, and I'm not happy about it. Eight confirmed residential break-ins in Joya in the last two months and we've got no witnesses and no physical evidence that leads us anywhere. Even so, I'm convinced that the guy, whoever he is, is pretty much an amateur. He kicks in the door and grabs what he can, but none of the stolen items have shown up yet. We'll get him eventually, but it's really annoying to have to explain to all these homeowners why we haven't caught him yet."

"You'll find him, dear," Linda said with serene confidence.

"Mother, you're always good for my self-esteem."

"Well, that's what mothers are for, Lea. Coffee, everyone?"

Jean drank a cup of coffee to ensure her alertness for the drive back, but begged off the delicious-looking flan. "I'm just tired from the day," she explained. "But it was a wonderful meal, Mrs. Hawkins. Thanks so much for inviting me."

"My daughter's lawyer is welcome anytime," Linda said warmly. "And it's Linda, remember?"

"I'll walk you out," Lea said.

The evening was mild, with a slight breeze that carried the scent of mesquite and pine. There was the faintest rustle of the low shrubs that surrounded the Hawkins's front porch. A city dweller all her life, Jean found the deep darkness and near-silence strange but oddly comforting, as if the earth were a small child safely huddled under dark blankets.

Lea opened the car door for her and Jean said, "It was nice of you to feed me twice in one day. Just for future reference, it's not a requirement for all attorney-client meetings."

"I disagree. You owe me two meals. So next time, you have to cook."

Jean could see Lea smiling at her in the darkness. "Fair enough. And don't worry about the deposition. You're going to be just fine."

"That's reassuring. Drive home carefully, okay?"

"I will."

* * *

It had been the best evening Jean had spent in a very long time. In fact, she couldn't remember the last time she had enjoyed herself so much. She couldn't decide if that realization cheered her or made her sad.

* * *

Jean unlocked the door to the house. The foyer was dazzlingly lit, the chandelier breaking the light into bright shards that sparkled across the two-story walls. A rope was tied to the chandelier and at the end of it Charlotte dangled in the noose, swaying just a little in the breeze from the open door. Her eyes were open and though Jean knew she was dead, Char said, "This is all your fault."

Jean jerked up in bed, icy cold again with the sweat freezing on her forehead. God, why did this keep happening? Why couldn't she be free of Charlotte?

You can't wipe out thirteen years in a few months, she reminded herself. *Give it time. Give yourself time.*

CHAPTER FIVE

Jean was busy with the file folder in her hands. She said into the speaker phone, "You're aware of the American Coroners Association report on excited delirium?"

"Well, yes, but there's no definitive proof that was the cause of death, even assuming the medical examiner agreed, which he hasn't. I'm not in a position to change the cause of death without further input."

The county coroner was dithering on and Jean's frustration was rising with every passing minute. The coroner was responsible for determining the cause of death for Mr. Rosales, but he relied on the medical examiner's autopsy findings to do so.

"All I'm asking you to do is review the situation with the medical examiner again in light of the ACA report," Jean said shortly. "And the sooner the better. We'll be in a settlement conference in six weeks and if there's going to be an amended death certificate, it needs to be soon."

The coroner prattled on for a while and Jean snapped the folder closed. She managed to end the conversation without yelling at him but she failed to get a promise from him to review the case. Monday was officially starting off badly.

She wandered out into the central office and saw Rita staring at a giant case file sitting in the middle of her desk. She raised dark, troubled eyes to Jean.

"What is it?" Jean asked sharply.

"The Lambert case. The former public works employee who was suing the county. Mr. Franklin just told me to close it and send the file to the shredder."

"What? It's an open case—" Jean began.

Rita interrupted. "Not any more. Did you read the paper this morning? There's been a burglar who has been hitting houses in Joya. He broke into Lambert's house last night but Lambert was home. The burglar killed him. Shot him dead."

Jean took a step back in shock, remembering the conversation at the Hawkins's dinner table Saturday evening. "Oh, my God."

"So I guess the case is over," Rita concluded.

"No, wait," Jean said reflexively.

"But Mr. Franklin told me to send it to the shredder," Rita repeated.

"We usually send case files to closed file storage for three years first, in case something else comes up," Jean said. "We don't need to send it to the shredder right away."

Rita glanced down the hall toward Franklin's office. "That's what he said to do."

"Besides which," Jean said, thinking aloud now, "the case may not be over. The action might survive his death."

"How?" Rita asked.

Jean liked that about Rita, that she wanted to know more rather than just follow instructions without question. Another curious mind. "For some types of lawsuits, the law permits the heirs to continue with the suit against the county," Jean explained. "It's called a survivorship statute. I'll have to do some research first. Give me the case file for now. I'll check it out and talk to Del later."

Rita said nervously, "But he said…"

"He just forgot about the survivorship statute I suppose, in the shock of finding out about Lambert's murder," Jean said, scrambling for an explanation. "If Del asks you about it, just tell him I took the file off your desk, okay?"

"Okay," Rita said. She seemed relieved but still worried.

Jean suited action to her words and hefted the single overstuffed file folder in both arms. She didn't want to get Rita into trouble but Del would probably regret his instructions in a few days and Jean would be able to give him the results of her research by then.

Just what I needed, another addition to the workload. But she didn't really mind very much, she acknowledged. The busier she was the less time she had to sit in her condo and wonder when the next nightmare was coming.

She dumped the file in one of her side chairs, which served as a place for overflow filing. She'd have to wait until after the Rosales deposition to get to the research on Lambert, but she was looking forward to it, in a way. It would help her get a good understanding on Franklin's litigation style as well as give her some information about the county public works department.

She smiled a little to herself. Snooping again.

She returned to her deposition prep for Rosales, but after a few minutes found herself thinking about dinner on Saturday at the Painted Horse Ranch. When was the last time she'd had a family dinner? She couldn't remember. She had trouble recalling the last time she'd had dinner with anyone but herself.

God, I have got to get a life.

She'd known, of course, that families like the Hawkinses existed but she'd never actually seen one up close. Her mother had treated her and her brother like annoyances, no more than barriers between her and her next husband. Boarding school had been a relief, with its structure and safety. She had at least been good at academics.

Life with Charlotte had been different, not about building a family but about building their careers. The only thing harder to forge than a successful career in private law practice was a career as a chef and restaurateur. It had gotten a little easier when Jean left her firm to join the Riverside County attorney's office. The hours in government work were less brutal and the job provided much better benefits though the pay was lower. Charlotte was an executive chef by then. With two solid incomes and Jean's insurance, Jean had thought it was time for them to think about getting pregnant.

Charlotte had refused to consider a baby and refused to even discuss why. Jean shook her head. Was that when the trouble started? More importantly, why was she going over this again?

She liked the Hawkins family. Linda was warm and kind, the mother she could have wished for growing up. Loren, for all he'd been through, was sweet and playful. And Lea, Lea was thoughtful and calm and had a—what would she call it? Maybe a grown-up tomboy charm.

Okay, she was attractive, Jean admitted. She thought about Lea's hands, the long, strong fingers. What color were her eyes? Jean couldn't remember. She'd have to look more carefully next time.

"Stop that right now," Jean said harshly. "I need a yoga class, not a relationship." A relationship makes promises that can't be kept, stealing your heart and then shredding it into bits, scattering the pieces so widely they can never be put back together again.

Restlessly, she pulled up the Tesóro *Banner* newspaper website and found the article about Fred Lambert's murder. It was brief, reading as if it had been written just before deadline. A neighbor had called the sheriff's office just before midnight to report a gunshot. The deputies had discovered Lambert shot to death in his kitchen, the door between kitchen and garage open. It was assumed that he'd interrupted the burglar who'd been busy in Joya recently. No suspects had been identified.

If Lea was feeling the stress before, Jean thought, it would be ten times worse now. A serial burglar was bad enough, but murder would undoubtedly put the investigation into a pressure cooker. She hoped Lea would still be able to focus at the deposition.

The deposition that was in less than two days, she reminded herself. Get back to work.

* * *

Discovery was the most tiresome part of any lawsuit and depositions were among the most tedious of discovery tools. Jean had always preferred research and writing, finding the best case law and crafting the best sentences to persuade a judge to rule in her client's favor.

But lawsuits usually turned on the facts, and discovery was all about determining what the facts were. She'd been through dozens of depositions in her career and they never got more interesting. Today, however, had been almost fun, an experience she could not remember having had before.

As she sat in the downtown coffee shop waiting for Lea to return with their drinks, she recalled her favorite moments of testimony.

* * *

The plaintiff's lawyer had asked early on, "Did you discuss what you were going to say today with anyone?"

Jean watched Lea hide her smile. She'd told Lea about this question during their prep.

"I'm not sure I understand," Lea had responded. "Are you asking me if I discussed what happened in the jail that evening with anyone or if I prepared for this deposition by consulting with my counsel?"

Plaintiff's lawyer snorted and it was Jean's turn to try not to grin. Lawyers hated it when witnesses asked them questions.

"Either one," he snapped.

Lea sat back easily in her chair and said, "I certainly discussed my testimony today with my attorney. And I've discussed the events at the jail several times with my staff, the board of county commissioners, the county risk manager and briefly with the press as well."

And what did that get you? Jean knew the question was an attempt to get the witness to deny discussing their testimony with anyone so that the attorney could catch them in a lie.

But the best moment was near the end when the plaintiff's lawyer asked, "You are aware that Mr. Rosales died while in your custody?"

"Yes."

"After being subjected to an unprovoked stun gun attack by your deputies?"

"Objection," Jean said quickly. "That mischaracterizes the prior testimony. The action was far from unprovoked."

He glared at her. "I'll rephrase. You are aware that Mr. Rosales died after the stun guns were used?"

"Yes."

"And yet you are denying any responsibility for his death?"

Jean watched Lea turn the question over. After a moment, Lea answered, "I wouldn't say that. I would say that I am denying any *fault* in connection with Mr. Rosales's death. He was in my custody. I am responsible for him in the greater sense of the word. But my deputies followed procedures and the procedures were sound. We did nothing wrong. We were not at fault. That doesn't mean I don't feel some responsibility."

Plaintiff's lawyer hadn't liked that answer one bit. It was all Jean could do not to applaud.

* * *

Lea brought the cardboard cup of coffee to the small table and said to Jean, "So, how do you think it went, Counselor?"

Jean sipped gratefully before answering. "It went really, really well. You did a great job."

Lea sat down, frowning. She was in full uniform, complete with service weapon and the tiny gold medal pinned to her chest. Jean saw the other late-afternoon patrons in the coffee shop steal glances at the sheriff. "You weren't worried when he went off on the procedures for removing prisoners from their cells?" Lea asked.

"Absolutely not. Remember, it's not a matter of whether the deputies did everything perfectly, that's not the legal standard in a lawsuit like this. The issue is whether your internal policies were adequate and after today, we're solid as a rock on this. If we don't get the case dismissed on a Motion for Summary Judgment, we'll be in a very strong settlement position."

"I always hate settling lawsuits when I don't think we've done anything wrong," Lea continued, still frowning.

"I understand. There is some economic point to it, usually based on how much it would cost the county to litigate the case in court as opposed to settling for a small amount. The stronger our legal position, the less we're likely to have to pay in settlement."

Lea drank from her cup and responded, "I get it. I just don't like it. I guess I'll just try to remember that the man did die while in our custody and his family is suffering, even if we weren't at fault." She sighed, and then continued, "Anyway, I appreciate all the work you did after Del Franklin dumped the case on you with no notice."

Jean murmured, "I didn't tell you Del dumped the case on me..."

Lea lifted an eyebrow. "No, you didn't. But I know Franklin a little, and it wasn't hard to figure out. But you did well to get ready in such a short period of time."

"I was fueled by that fantastic meal your mother fed me on Saturday," Jean said lightly. "Did your dad get home all right?"

"Yep. Mom said he ate about a gallon or so of chili when he got home after ten o'clock and then he spent half the night up with well-deserved indigestion."

Lea looked tired, the skin around her eyes stretched more tightly than Jean remembered. She didn't think it was the deposition that had stressed her so much. Lea had been cool and professional, just as Jean had expected. "How's the murder case coming?"

A sharp glance from Lea surprised her. Wasn't Jean supposed to talk about it? Carefully, Lea said, "We're working on it. Why do you ask?"

Cops, Jean thought in exasperation. Answering a question with a question. They were worse than lawyers. "Did you know the murder victim, Lambert, was suing the county?"

Sitting back in her chair, Lea said, "No, I didn't, actually. Tell me more about that."

"He was a former county employee in public works. He was suing the board of county commissioners claiming he'd been wrongfully fired."

"Was he?" Lea asked.

"I don't know. I haven't had time to read the case file yet. And the lawsuit wouldn't have anything to do with his murder anyway." At Lea's tightening mouth she added, "Would it?"

"I don't think so," Lea acknowledged. "The murder looks like the work of our Joya burglar. But he's never made a mistake before like this, entering a house with someone home and, obviously, he's never used a weapon. Changes in the MO always bother me."

Jean saw Lea watching her. Lea's face was thoughtful. What was she thinking, whether or not she could trust Jean with the details of the investigation? Or something else, something more personal, perhaps?

Jean lifted her gaze to Lea's eyes. She had hazel eyes, Jean decided. Her eyes were looking gray-green now with the khaki uniform. The single lock of wavy hair was threatening to escape over her forehead.

Lea Hawkins is not an option, Jean told herself firmly. Even if she's available, you're not, so stop looking at her.

Suddenly Lea asked, "May I ask if you're busy on Sunday?"

Despite her best intentions, Jean answered quickly, "I'm not. What's up?"

"It's the Green Chile Festival," Lea said. "You're new in town and you should have someone introduce you to the local celebrations. We close off several streets downtown and there are booths with food, a few local restaurants roasting chiles, usually a mariachi band or two. Sound like fun?"

Was this a date? A ripple of indecision shuddered through her, then she took a deep breath. Time to come clean, at least a little.

But before she could speak, Lea said, "You look a little shell-shocked. Did I say something wrong?"

"No, it's just that I'm not sure exactly what you—I mean, I'm your lawyer, or at least officially so and we, ah…".

Lea said softly, "It's all right, Jean. I go every year and I thought you'd like it. I'm not asking you on a date. But it would be nice to just hang out. Wouldn't it?"

Jean relaxed. She could use a friend, God knew, and she liked Lea. It would be fine. She admired Lea for taking a chance by asking her. In the end all she could say was, "It does sound like fun. What time?"

* * *

Sunday was unseasonably warm, the sun bright gold and the mountains in the west clear and blue. Jean debated briefly over what to wear and then gave up worrying. She found her favorite walking shorts and paired them with a camp shirt. Tying a sweater around her shoulders in case she was out later in the day, Jean worked very hard not to think about anything other than having a fun time. They were just hanging out, she reminded herself. Friends spending time together.

She walked over a couple of blocks from her downtown condo to meet Lea at the corner of Main and Fifth, the sunshine pleasantly hot on her shoulders. After a minute she spotted Lea, standing and talking to a uniformed officer who was stationed beside a wooden barrier. She shook his hand when she spotted Jean and walked over to meet her. Out of uniform, Lea was dressed in jeans, boots and a sleeveless western shirt, her arms long and tan and lean.

Stop it, Jean said. She was getting tired of telling herself that.

"Hi," Lea greeted her cheerfully. "You look dressed for the day."

Jean gestured toward the officer Lea had been talking to a moment before. "Is there a problem?"

"Not at all. I'm just checking in. The Tesóro City Police Department is in charge of the event, but we always send some deputies over to help with traffic control."

They fell into an easy stroll, wandering among the pedestrians crowding the street. "Are you really always on duty?" Jean asked.

"Pretty much," Lea responded. "I don't mind. It's part of the job. I certainly knew what I was getting into when I ran for office."

They stopped to buy a couple of empanadas and ate as they walked. The pastry fell in delicious flakes around the savory, seasoned ground beef. "I meant to ask you, how did your father escape having the law enforcement career the rest of his family had?" Jean asked.

After swallowing a mouthful of empanada, Lea answered, "Vietnam. He's got a Purple Heart for a shoulder wound that prevented him from passing the physical. I think he was okay with it, actually. He really, really wanted to marry Mom and it's a lot easier to have a normal family life as a rancher than as a cop."

Is that why you're single? Jean wanted to ask.

Licking their fingers clean from the empanada crumbs, they browsed booths filled with a variety of items for sale, from homemade jellies to brightly colored woven purses. For a few minutes they paused to listen to a mariachi band, bright trumpets and guitars making the atmosphere on the sidewalk a fiesta.

Soon after they resumed their walk the spicy, earthy smell of roasted chiles swirled around them, luring them by the nose toward the large metal cylinders tended by men wearing bright red aprons and wielding long metal tongs.

"My God, that smells wonderful," Jean exclaimed.

Lea grinned at her. "It smells like home to me. There is nothing like a roasted green chile."

"Are green chiles a different kind of pepper from red chiles?" Jean asked.

Lea looked at her quizzically. "I thought you were from Texas."

"Where I come from, chili means 'chili con carne.' And in Texas, it's always about the beef. Sometimes the chili is made without the meat, but with beans instead. But 'chili' has nothing to do with chile peppers per se. Other than the occasional jalapeño."

"Well, in that case, let me help you on your way to becoming a citizen of the Southwest." Lea gave her a lopsided grin. "Red chiles are green chiles that were left on the chile plant long enough to ripen, simple as that. The flavors of red and green chiles are very different from each other and to complicate matters, you can have your chiles smoked or not. For example, a jalapeño pepper that's been smoked is called a chipotle."

Jean asked happily, "This conversation is making me hungry. Is it too soon for lunch?"

Lea laughed. "It's never too soon for lunch. I recommend a nice medium-rare burger with roasted green chiles on top. Sound good?"

"Yes, but if you don't eat yours fast enough, you may go hungry. All food left unattended is subject to possible confiscation by an officer of the court."

"I am forewarned," Lea said with mock solemnity.

They bought their burgers, and then found two seats at one of the picnic tables set up nearby. There were lots of families, people casually dressed in jeans or shorts for the sunny day at the end of summer. Lea said, "I'm reluctant to leave my burger in your care, but I need to go get drinks. Do you want a beer?"

Jean said, "I don't drink. Water is fine."

Lea returned with the bottles of water, the ice still clinging to the sides. After twisting off the cap, Jean drank deeply. Then she took a healthy bite of the juicy burger.

"Are the chiles too hot for you?" Lea asked.

"After your mother's chili, they're mild as baby food."

"Interesting that you should say that. I'm pretty sure Mom fed green chiles to us in our Gerber's strained peas to acclimate us."

Jean smiled. "I don't doubt it."

They ate in happy silence for a moment. Then Lea said, "May I ask you a very personal question?"

Jean almost laughed at her formal politeness, then wondered what the question might be. "Yes, you may."

"Are you an alcoholic?"

Jean put her half-eaten burger down on the paper plate. "You're assuming that if I don't drink I'm an alcoholic?"

"No, I'm not assuming anything," she said gently. "That's why I asked."

"Point taken. Is it important?"

"If you're asking me whether it matters to me or not, it doesn't. I thought if I knew, I'd quit offering you adult beverages and make it easier on you, that's all."

Jean heard no note of condescension or judgment in her tone. She replied, "No, I'm not an alcoholic. But I'm pretty certain that my mother is. I don't really like the taste of alcohol very much and I didn't see the point in taking a chance on continuing the family tradition." She gestured at the bottles of water. "But that doesn't mean you can't have a beer. It doesn't bother me if other people are drinking."

Lea shrugged. "If there's any chance I might need to work, I'd rather not have alcohol in my system. I usually wait until I leave town to have a drink."

Jean picked up her burger again. The mild, freshly smoked spice of the green chiles complemented the succulent beef perfectly and Jean tried not to wolf down her meal. "Do you leave town a lot?" she asked.

She'd thought the question innocuous, but Lea hesitated a long moment. "I used to," she admitted. "I was involved with a woman who lived in Denver and I drove up almost every other weekend for years."

Treading carefully, Jean said, "Long-distance relationships are tough, I imagine."

"Denver is only a hundred miles or so north of here. It was more of a medium-distance relationship."

Lea was trying for lightness of tone, but Jean heard regret behind the words. "What happened?" she finally asked.

"I couldn't leave San Carlos County, obviously," Lea answered. "Her career was important to her too and she needed to be in Denver. We made it work pretty well for quite a while and then not so well for a longer while. When she got transferred to Atlanta, it was time to finish it between us. We were together a long time, but ending the relationship was pretty much mutual."

"Almost ten years, your mother told me."

Lea gave her the half smile. "Mother is very chatty. I should know that by now."

"Then she probably told you I had a partner for thirteen years."

Lea fiddled with her water bottle a moment, then she said, "She mentioned it. A chef, she said."

"Yes."

"It wasn't a good ending." Lea made it a statement rather than a question.

"I didn't tell your mother that."

"No." Lea's voice was gentle. "I can see it in your face."

Jean stared at her. The hazel eyes were more light brown today, almost golden. Was her pain obvious to everyone? Jean wondered. She thought she had hidden it rather well, but perhaps she was fooling herself.

Jean said, "No, it wasn't a good ending. She left me."

Before she heard Lea's response, the conversation was interrupted by a loud shout, followed by the wail of a crying child. Jean spotted a little girl, perhaps four or five, standing near one of the hot metal chile roasters. She jumped to her feet but Lea was faster. She had the child scooped into her arms in a few seconds.

"Are you hurt, honey?" Lea asked gently.

The man standing nearby brandishing tongs exclaimed, "I just managed to keep her from touching it. I think I scared her, though."

Lea inspected the child's hands and arms, but apparently didn't see any burns. Jean looked around, expecting to see a frantic parent or two, but no one seemed nearby.

Lea was making comforting noises, saying, "You're okay now. Everything's okay."

The girl said, "I'm not 'posed to talk to strangers."

"That's a good rule." Lea set her on the ground. "My name is Lea, what's yours?"

"Cheryl. But I can't talk to you."

"Hmmm. Did your mother tell you about police officers?"

"Yes." The little girl's eyes grew round.

Lea dug her badge from her jeans pocket and showed it to Cheryl. "It's okay to talk to me. I'm the sheriff, see? It's just like being a police officer."

"You can't be a p'liceman. You're a girl."

Lea smiled. "Girls make very good police officers sometimes. Can you tell me where your mother or dad is?"

The tears started again. "I don't know. They losted me."

Lea picked her up again. She said reassuringly, "Don't worry, we'll find them."

She and Jean canvassed the picnic area without success. Lea was all gentle kindness with Cheryl, but Jean could see her anger beginning to build in the flush of Lea's face. How had the girl's parents managed to let her get so far away?

They widened the search radius. At length, Jean asked, "Do you want me to get another officer and see if they can help you look?"

"Probably a good idea," Lea acknowledged. A moment later she said sharply, "Wait a minute, Jean."

Across the street a man and woman stood arguing on the sidewalk, drawing the uncomfortable glances of those around them. Passersby were giving them a wide berth as their voices rose.

"Don't fuck with me!" the man yelled. "You act like I'm a moron or something! I know what you're doing with him!"

"You don't know jack shit!" the woman screamed back at him.

Lea turned to Jean and said tersely, "Take her." She handed the girl into Jean's arms.

She crossed over to the angry couple and Jean felt a tiny shiver of anxiety. What was she worried about? Surely Lea could take care of herself. But despite the reassurance, she drew closer as if somehow to protect Lea's back.

She couldn't hear the words, but after a moment Lea's calm voice gave way to a sudden cry as the woman sprang away, rushing toward Jean with her arms widespread. Cheryl cried out, "Mommy!" and Jean handed the child over after glancing over to see Lea's nod.

"Oh, baby, where were you?" the woman cried.

Jean barely muttered, "If you'd been paying even a little bit of attention, you'd know, wouldn't you?"

The woman didn't hear her, fortunately, consumed with comforting her daughter. Behind them the man was yelling at Lea now, gesturing wildly with his arms and looking more and more threatening. Jean suffered a moment of indecision—should she go for help?

"It's none of your fucking business!" the man yelled at Lea, and Jean made her choice. She moved around them circling toward the man's back. What she expected to do if things went badly she had no idea, but at least she wasn't leaving Lea alone.

Lea said calmly, "You need to walk away for a few minutes, sir, and calm down. Now."

"Fuck you!" he screamed again and Jean wondered at Lea's self-control. Lea was standing carefully just out of the man's range, watching his hands. Jean was watching them too as he abruptly turned, shifting his weight and bringing his arm back to throw the punch.

"Lea!" Jean yelled.

But Lea was already moving out of the way, avoiding the blow almost gracefully and seizing the arm passing near her. With a motion too fast for Jean to follow, she had the man's arm pinned behind his back. A moment later she put her leg into his knee from behind and dropped him to kneel on the pavement.

Lea said firmly, "You're under arrest. Do not resist or you're going to get hurt."

He struggled briefly anyway. Lea tightened her grip and lifted his arm another inch. He winced in pain and cursed her loudly.

Jean knew what to do now. She ran straight for the nearest uniform.

"Sheriff Hawkins needs help." It was all she had to say and right away half a dozen officers were running toward them.

The next few minutes were all confusion and loud voices, tempered only by Lea's cool orders as she took charge of everyone else. When a Tesóro police officer with multiple stripes on his sleeves arrived on the scene, Lea gracefully turned the prisoner and the situation over to him, coming to stand near Jean.

"Sorry about this," she said quietly to Jean. "This was not the way I wanted to spend the afternoon."

"Not your fault. You're okay?"

"I'm fine. He's drunk and in a whole lot of trouble. Cheryl's mom is in some trouble too. Not a good situation for anyone."

"No," Jean agreed. "But the important thing is that the little girl's all right."

"Well, sort of," Lea said unhappily. "If they decide to book Mom on child neglect charges, Cheryl will be with a relative tonight if she's lucky or foster care if she's not."

"Oh." Jean remembered the consequences visited on children by their self-centered parents.

"It may not come to that," Lea said and Jean realized she was trying to reassure her. "The girl wasn't hurt and her mother will probably just be issued a misdemeanor ticket. Mom will be able to take her home. Dad, of course, is in a lot more trouble."

"Attempted assault," Jean muttered with satisfaction. "Public intoxication and child neglect. Resisting arrest too, I imagine."

"Yep. Overnight in jail, at least. I'm going to have to go down to Tesóro Police HQ and make a statement. And so will you, I'm afraid. Again, I'm really sorry about all this."

"I just wish we'd gotten to finish our burgers first," Jean sighed.

* * *

The sun was setting by the time they left the downtown police building. The few clouds hanging over the mountains caught garish shades of orange and peach as the peaks seemed to reach up to pull the sun down behind them. The air had cooled and Jean was glad for her sweater.

"Do you want dinner?" Lea asked. "I feel bad that you didn't get all of your lunch."

"I could certainly afford to miss a meal or two," Jean said ruefully.

With a steady look, Lea said, "Not as far as I can see."

Was she flirting or just being nice? Jean wondered. But she had anticipated the dinner invitation and she had already decided that she needed to go home. Lea was just a little too appealing, kind and thoughtful and strong. And she was a client and Jean was not in the market for a relationship.

"I'm a little tired. I think I'll just go on home, but thanks," she said.

Lea might have been a little disappointed, but Jean couldn't read her. Lea said, "Okay. I'll walk you back."

"You don't have to do that."

Giving her the crooked half smile Lea said, "Yes, I know."

They walked all the way back to Jean's building in silence, a comfortable quiet. Jean couldn't keep from comparing her to Charlotte, who would talk nonstop in her manic moods and refused to interact in her depressed phases. There had been sparks at times, certainly, but there had never been a comfortable silence between them of any kind.

When they arrived at Jean's building, Lea said, "Guess I'll have to give you a rain check for next year's festival."

Jean said dryly, "I'll put it on my calendar. With my busy social schedule, I get booked up so quickly."

"Well, I knew that," Lea said. "That's why I wanted to get my request in early. Have a good evening."

The sun had dipped below the jagged horizon of the hills in the west, turning the sky above them deep crimson and scarlet. Jean tried to feel relieved as she watched Lea walk back down the street toward her truck.

But the effort was unsuccessful. She needed to get a handle on this attraction and soon. Lea Hawkins is not an option, Jean reminded herself once again.

CHAPTER SIX

Jean was washing her hands in the ladies' room at work when Carolyn Forsythe emerged from a stall and joined her at the sinks.

"Commissioner," Jean greeted her.

"Ms. McAllister. Jean, isn't it? I haven't had a chance to tell you how pleased we are that you came to work at San Carlos County. Del thinks very highly of you."

Does he? Jean wondered cynically, but said only, "I'm very glad to be here, I truly am."

"Yes, we believe we're the premier county in Colorado," Carolyn continued, "and our staff is one of the reasons why. We know you came very highly recommended from, hmm, California, correct?"

Carolyn was treating her less like a professional colleague and more like a well-recommended caterer, but Jean had been employed by local government long enough to know how to play the game.

"Yes, California," she confirmed. "And I must say, both the weather and the traffic are wonderful here in comparison."

Carolyn beamed at her happily. "Yes, people think Colorado is so cold, but really, almost all of the snow is in the mountains. Most of the time it's really nice and mild on the Front Range."

Jean dried her hands and applied some lotion. This ladies' room served only the county offices, not the general public, so the commissioners' staff made sure there was always air freshener and hand lotion available.

"Are you a native of Colorado?" Jean asked. She'd been here long enough to know how many people living in the state had been born somewhere else.

Carolyn looked almost embarrassed. "No, but I've lived here since Andy and I got married and his company transferred him, oh, it's been almost thirty years ago. We raised our kids here, so it certainly feels like home."

"Of course it does," Jean said, wondering how much more small talk she could manage. "Are your children still here?"

"Cindy's up at college in Greeley, Colorado State. Andy Junior is with the Peace Corps in South America, teaching English in Peru." She sighed deeply and added, "We're so proud of him."

Something in her tone made Jean doubt her words but she said, "You should be. What a fine thing for him to do."

"Yes," Carolyn said, still sounding dubious. Apparently she wanted her son home pursuing his corporate—or perhaps political—career.

Jean said, "Well, back to work. It was nice to see you."

Carolyn laid a hand on her arm. She said, "Wait. Has Del told you about the Harvest Moon Party?"

"No," Jean said, trying to suppress her surprise. Why on earth would her boss ask her about a party?

"It's sort of a social event for high-ranking county staff, elected officials and, of course, prominent people in both political parties. It's, well, rather expected that the department heads and their deputies attend." She gave Jean an interesting smile, partly imperious yet shy as well. "You really should attend. It's Saturday night. There is always a theme of some kind."

"A costume party?" Jean tried not to sound dismayed.

Carolyn laughed lightly. "Not really, but you do want to dress appropriately. It's a western theme this year because Lou Hawkins is hosting it at his ranch. He's Sheriff Hawkins's father, you know. Very politically active family, the Hawkinses. Well, her parents, really. The sheriff doesn't go in as much for politics, but of course anyone who holds elective office has to be involved to a certain extent…"

Her voice trailed off and before she could gather energy for another topic, Jean said, "Sounds like fun. I'm sure Del just forgot to tell me about it."

Carolyn patted her arm in a friendly way. "I'm sure that's true. He's so very busy. We do keep him running."

"Yes. Did you hear about the former public works employee who was suing us, Fred Lambert?"

Carolyn's face fell. "Oh, yes, poor man. I know Hayward really resented him, but how sad! His poor wife, finding him like that. Del did tell us that would end the lawsuit, of course."

Did he? Jean wondered why Del was so determined to bury Lambert's lawsuit so quickly. Maybe it was time to look at the file sitting in her office.

"I'll see you on Saturday night," Carolyn called cheerfully as Jean left the restroom.

* * *

Where on earth was she going to find an outfit to go with a western theme? She could manage the cowboy boots. She and Charlotte occasionally rode early in their relationship though it had been years since she'd worn the boots for their intended purpose. But boots alone weren't going to be enough. What else could she wear? Her jeans hardly seemed suitable.

She was still pondering the problem when she passed by her paralegal's desk. Struck by sudden inspiration she asked, "Rita, you've never been to the Harvest Moon Party, have you?"

"Oh, no!" Rita exclaimed. "It's only for elected officials and department heads and people like that. Why?"

"Because Commissioner Forsythe pretty much just ordered me to attend and I have no idea what to wear."

Rita tapped her fingers lightly against her keyboard. "What's the party theme this year?"

"Western, Commissioner Forsythe said. It's at the Hawkins's ranch."

Rita smiled. "Well, that's good news. At least the food and the music will be good. The word is that Linda Hawkins knows how to throw a party."

"Isn't the party always a good one?" Jean asked.

Rita laughed. "Goodness, no! The elected officials sort of rotate hosting duties and two years ago it was Netta Telford, the county clerk." She lowered her voice. "She had it at the convention center downtown and everybody who went was complaining about the band playing 'Macarena' over and over. *And* they had a caterer who used Cheez Whiz on the canapés. Seriously."

Jean shuddered at the thought of Cheez Whiz and the paralegal chuckled again. Rita had always been so serious when they were working together that Jean welcomed her laughter. "Look," Jean said impulsively, "I really don't know where to go shopping yet. If I buy lunch, would you go shopping with me, to try to find something for me to wear? If you're not busy," she added hastily.

Rita looked surprised for a moment, then smiled. "I love shopping," she admitted, "and the peanut butter sandwich I brought for lunch can certainly wait. Come get me when you're ready. I have a couple of places in mind. There's a great vintage clothing store a couple of blocks away that might be perfect."

The vintage store, Yesterday's Glory, yielded the perfect blouse: a calico with a single ruffle down the placket and a western-style yoke. They couldn't find a skirt, but Rita had a plan.

"Just go with a denim skirt, long enough to get to the top of your boots," she said as they ate their burritos. "And not too dark blue, you want it to go with the blue in the shirt."

In genuine admiration, Jean said, "You have a knack for this. Maybe you should drop by my condo every morning and pick out my outfits."

"You look fine," Rita said seriously. "Very professional."

"Hmm. Is that your way of saying I look boring?"

Rita ducked her head, pushing her fork through the refried beans. "No, it's just...I know you haven't worked in Colorado before and we're kinda more, you know, casual here."

Gently amused, Jean said, "I'll keep that in mind. Perhaps I could leave the suits at home on days when I don't have a meeting."

"I'm not trying to tell you what to do—" Rita began to protest, but Jean cut her off. "No, I didn't take it that way at all," she said kindly. "I appreciate that you're looking out for me, I do."

Rita sighed, apparently relieved. "It's a nice place, Painted Horse Ranch."

"I know," Jean responded. "I've been there." At Rita's curious look, Jean explained her visit on the day she went out to do the deposition preparation.

"Oh," Rita said. After a long pause, she said, "So you met Loren, I guess."

Was there a faint blush on her cheeks? Jean suppressed her smile and answered, "Yes. He was very charming. A handsome man. It's very sad about what happened to him."

Rita looked genuinely distressed. "It was so terrible for him. I'm—I'm glad he's doing better."

"You know him, then?"

Rita nodded. "We went to high school together, Joya High. He was a couple of years ahead of me. I'm sure he doesn't remember me."

Maybe so, Jean thought, maybe not. But remembering Loren's flirting with her, she was willing to bet he might very much want to know Rita now. She'd just have to come up with some way to renew their acquaintance. Maybe Lea would have an idea.

She'd managed not to think much about Lea being at the party, but now she realized she was looking forward to seeing her again. Jean sighed. She was going to need a strategy for dealing with her emotions. The problem was made more difficult since she couldn't tell what Lea might be feeling.

Friendship, she reminded herself, that was what she was aiming for here. The sheriff and her family obviously had a lot of influence in county affairs and it was certainly in her best long-term employment interest to maintain a good relationship with Lea Hawkins.

This tactic would work beautifully as soon as she could get a grip on what was, she admitted, her growing personal interest in Lea. Jean recognized it for what it was: she had just been alone too long. Even before it ended with Charlotte, she'd been without a lover for a long while. She would be able to overcome this. It would be all right. It was just temporary.

She just wished she could stop feeling so cold all the time.

* * *

As Jean walked up to the barn at Painted Horse Ranch, she remembered the greeting she'd gotten from the dogs on her last visit. She wondered where Wyatt and Doc had been sequestered for the duration of the party. The yard in front of the house was full of cars and trucks and SUVs, carefully parked away from Linda Hawkins's desert garden, protected by ropes strung along poles around the borders. The path to the barn had been well lit by strings of white lights draped along the fence rails of the corral. The air was filled with the woody sweet scents of piñon and mesquite.

The barn doors were fully open, bright light pouring like a silver waterfall across the sandy ground. The light didn't quite reach the porch, which lay in deep shadows. The lights were off in the house too.

Music rippled out of the barn, guitars and a fiddle. Someone was singing an old Johnny Cash tune in a reasonable baritone and Jean felt herself drawn into the light, the music and the voices.

She smoothed her denim skirt, which was the perfect color blue, and stepped into the barn. She didn't know where the horses had been stabled, but the barn was clean as an operating room, scrubbed and pristine. There were curtains hung in front of mock windows, each tied back with red kerchiefs. The massive food table was covered with a red-and-white checkered tablecloth and laid with dozens of dishes. Jean cruised closer and did a survey: tamales and what looked to be Linda's near-lethal chili, piles of tortillas and chips and salsa and queso, a huge neat pile of smoked beef brisket alongside soft white sandwich buns, all supplemented with the required vegetable and fruit trays. The drinks were at another table, bottles and cans iced down in huge galvanized tubs. At one end of the barn, the Hawkins had built a small stage for the musicians. The quartet of two guitars, drummer and singer had segued into a Garth Brooks song.

In the center of the room people were dancing, cowboy boots shuffling on the floor. Jean scanned the room as she looked for people she might know.

Board chairman Jaime Fontana was in one corner talking to a couple of men Jean didn't recognize. Del Franklin was with a woman Jean assumed was his wife, chatting to Carolyn Forsythe and a man who must be her husband. Jean wondered how awkward that conversation might be. She didn't spot Hayward Lyons, but she did see the county clerk, the treasurer, even the public trustee, all working the room, shaking hands, greeting friends and probably foes as well. County employees crowded the barn too, the head of the purchasing department, information technology manager, the public affairs officer all present and accounted for.

Jean took a couple of tamales, avoided the chile, and slid to the corner to watch the room while she ate. She peeled the husks from the tamales and enjoyed the savory pork filling surrounded by sweet corn masa. Jaime Fontana stayed in one place, still talking to the same two men. Major campaign contributors? County political party officials? She knew Fontana was term-limited, so she wondered if he was planning for his next job. Maybe a state representative slot?

By contrast, Carolyn Forsythe was walking around to every group of people in the room with Del Franklin at her side. Forsythe's husband and Franklin's wife trailed behind them like remoras clinging to a pair of sharks. The analogy amused Jean and she laughed quietly to herself.

She finally spotted Hayward Lyons standing near the bandstand. He was drinking a beer and was near a small group of people, but his eyes were on someone across the room. As Jean followed his gaze, she saw that he was watching Carolyn and Del. Even across the room Jean could see that his eyes were alight with animosity.

Was his dislike for Carolyn? Or Del? Was he jealous, or was there something else?

Jean finished her tamales and listened to the music for a while. At length she saw Lea on the dance floor, dancing with a tall man whose hair was a wavy iron gray. They were talking easily and Jean could guess the man was Lou Hawkins.

He was a good dancer, easy and smooth, and Jean could see where Lea got her grace of movement. The man said something that made Lea laugh and Jean felt a pinprick of envy. She suppressed it ruthlessly and went in search of other people to talk to somewhere else.

She greeted Del, who seemed too distracted to say more than a brief hello. Carolyn was in a more chatty mood, introducing Jean to her husband and inquiring brightly if Jean was there by herself.

"Yes," Jean acknowledged. "I'm alone."

After making it a point to welcome every county official she could track down, she finally located Linda Hawkins. "It's a wonderful party," Jean greeted her.

Linda was resplendent in a full-skirted dress, tastefully studded with rhinestones. She looked like a rodeo queen and Jean told her so.

Linda laughed. "I'll tell you a secret, Jean. I just love giving parties. I was going to try to talk the board into letting us host this one every year but Lea pitched a fit. She really hates all of this political hoo-haw."

"Do you enjoy it? The political hoo-haw, that is," Jean asked.

"Not really. Lou loves it, but I just like food and music and people and parties. What can I say?"

"Well, you've done a fine job with this one," Jean said again. "The tamales were great, by the way."

"My mother's recipe," Linda said, clearly pleased.

"Would that be Rosalea?"

Linda gave her an appraising look. "Ah. Lea told you about her?"

"She did. I think she's very proud of the Hispanic part of her heritage, though I'm not sure she loves the name."

Linda's laugh echoed through the barn. "I'm pretty sure you're right. It was my compromise with Lou. I got to name my daughter Rosalea and he got to call her Lea. It suits her better anyway."

"It does," Jean agreed. "Thanks again for the invitation. It's good to see you."

She began to move off, but Linda said, "Don't be a stranger, Jean. You're welcome at our ranch any time."

Jean smiled her thanks. It still felt odd to her to be welcomed in another family's home.

There was no one else she needed to see and Jean began to wonder if it was too early in the evening to think about leaving.

The song the band had been playing ended. Couples separated and clapped as the musicians announced a brief break. Most of the dancers peeled off toward either the food or drink tables.

Someone took her elbow gently and she turned to see Lea.

"Hello," Lea said quietly. "I'm glad you decided to come."

The touch of Lea's fingers on her arm got all of Jean's attention. Jean carefully detached herself. She said, "It looked like you were having a good time on the dance floor."

Lea was wearing the dressiest cowgirl shirt Jean had ever seen, black with huge red flowers that matched her red boots. She was wearing tiny gold hoops in her ears. Around her throat she had tied a thin red silk kerchief. It looked for a moment like a slender line of blood across her throat and Jean had to shake the image from her head.

"I always have a good time dancing with my father," Lea said.

"I thought it might be him," Jean acknowledged. "You have his eyes."

At that moment, Lou Hawkins joined them, carrying a plate in one hand and a beer in the other. Lea stole one of his carrot sticks. "Dad, this is Jean McAllister."

"I'm happy to meet you," he said in a deep bass voice. "Lea tells us you're her new lawyer. I understand Linda almost killed you with her chili last time."

"I survived pretty well. This is quite a party you're putting on."

Lou smiled, the lines around his eyes and mouth deep and sharply cut. His face looked as if he had faced into the wind for a long time. He was wearing a cream-colored western shirt under a leather vest and a bolo tie with a turquoise slide adding a splash of color. On his wrist was a handsome woven horsehair bracelet. He said, "Well, it's just for my wife. She likes to throw a party every now and then."

Lea grinned at him. "Oh, please. You just met Jean, so you don't know her well enough to lie to her. You love doing this stuff."

He pointed the beer bottle at his daughter. "I'm just doing it for you, so be nice."

Lea shook her head at Jean. "He's lying again. He eats up all this glad-handing and schmoozing."

"Oh, hush now. I just like to keep my hand in, you know that."

"You know all these people?" Jean interjected.

"Most of 'em," Lou acknowledged. "I've known Hayward Lyons for quite a few years and Carolyn Forsythe longer than that. And I knew Jaime when he was a chubby little kid with skinned knees."

Lea said, "All right, go on and work the room. You know you want to. Thanks for the dance, Dad."

He lifted a thick, wiry eyebrow at her. "Trying to get rid of me?"

Jean watched Lea flush a little, but she answered calmly, "Yes. You're practically twitching. Go on."

He chuckled, a deep rumbling sound. "It's nice to meet you, Ms. McAllister. See you again soon, I hope." Coming from him the sentiment sounded less like a request and more like a royal command.

He moved off with purpose toward a group near the bandstand. Jean said, "He's quite the dynamic personality."

Lea said wryly, "You have no idea."

"Is Loren here?"

Lea glanced around. "Yes, somewhere. He may be hanging out with the musicians. He's quite the guitar player and he likes to pick up tips."

A little hesitantly, Jean asked, "Do you think he might be interested in meeting someone?"

"Meeting someone? You mean a someone of the female persuasion?"

"Yes. My paralegal mentioned that she remembered him from high school and I thought she seemed, well, interested."

Lea looked thoughtful. "That might just be a good idea. Let me think about how we might arrange it so it doesn't seem too much like a setup. I don't want Loren thinking I'm afraid he can't get a date on his own but he could certainly use a little friendly assistance."

"Okay. Let me know what I can do to help. Rita seems very nice and I'd love to be able to give them a chance."

"That's nice of you," Lea said quietly. "Look, do you want some water or something?"

"I could use a beverage," Jean said, realizing she was no longer in a hurry to leave.

"I'm a little thirsty too," Lea said. "Why don't you go outside to get away from the noise a minute and let me bring us something to drink?"

Lea seemed back to her usual friendly and relaxed self, so Jean said, "Sure."

She wandered out of the barn, crossing to the back porch. Sitting down on the steps, she watched the huge yellow moon hang like a giant paper lantern in the sky above the barn. Then she watched Lea cross the sandy yard between them, two brown bottles dangling from one hand. They looked like beer bottles and Jean realized she must be frowning when Lea reached her. Lea reassured her saying, "Don't worry, you'll like it."

Lea handed her an icy bottle and Jean asked, "What is it?"

"Root beer, believe it or not," Lea answered. "It's made by a local microbrewery. They only sell it in Colorado. Try it, I really do think you'll enjoy it."

Jean took a long drink and nodded. "It's good. Not too sweet. I can really taste the anise."

"Glad you like it."

They sat in the evening, the voices from the barn muted and far away. Jean thought again how comfortable it was just to be quiet with Lea, a feeling she'd never had before with anyone else. That's how friends are together, she congratulated herself.

The band began again, the singer insisting that even if he'd known how the love affair would end, he would have loved her anyway. Jean didn't believe it. If she'd known how it would end with Charlotte, she would have chosen a different path. The good times in the beginning weren't worth all the pain that had come later, the pain she was suffering still.

After tipping her bottle to drain the last swallow, Lea set it on the bottom step of the porch. She stood up and offered her hand to Jean. Then she said softly, "Dance with me."

Jean looked up at Lea, pale moonlight silvering her hair, thinking she should refuse, knowing she would not. She stood and lifted her arms, ready to lay them casually on Lea's shoulders. But Lea stepped in and circled Jean's waist with her right arm, taking Jean's other hand as if they were about to waltz.

Lea led gracefully and Jean was able to follow her easily. Across the sandy soil they moved together. As the song ended, the band immediately began another, an old Anne Murray tune. Jean remembered the lyrics about two old lovers reuniting after many years apart. The singer began the chorus.

I need one more dance
With my arms around you
As they should have been
All along.
Give me one more chance
To be your love

Give me one last chance
One more dance.

Jean put her head against Lea's shoulder, feeling the slight play of muscle beneath the skin as they moved together. Lea's hand, holding her lightly in the small of her back, was warm. Jean could feel the strength of the fingers through the fabric of her shirt.

As the song continued, Jean's hand slid up slightly to touch the soft waves of hair that fell just over Lea's collar in the back. Jean shut her eyes to try to let the music and the dancer take her far away from the loneliness and pain of her past. She made an effort to be here, in this moment only, but Charlotte's memory wouldn't let her go.

There would be no more chances for them, no last dance. Whatever was in her past was written and no word could be changed. She had only this moment, this dance.

She had to let Charlotte go. She had to forgive herself, to forgive Charlotte too. She'd gone over all the time they were together, trying to think what she could have done differently, but it didn't matter now.

It was time to say goodbye. She said the word to herself, silently.

Jean let Lea guide her to the end of the song, then realized how closely she was clinging. Embarrassed, she stepped away as Lea dropped her arms.

"It's all right," Lea said, very quietly.

"What's all right?" Jean asked.

"Whatever it is that's making you sad," Lea answered. "Whatever it is, it will be all right."

Jean didn't know how to respond to that, so instead she reached over and touched Lea lightly on the arm. "Thank you for the dance."

"No, thank you," Lea responded. "It's been a very long time since I got to dance with a beautiful woman."

Warmth flooded Jean's face in the cool evening air. "I'm hardly beautiful, unless you're into a kind of geeky girl look. I imagine it was a little cute when I was twenty, but it's not exactly endearing at forty."

Lea answered, "You're wrong about that. Twenty has its charm, but I prefer the company of grown-up women myself."

"Grown-up women are a lot more complicated than twenty-year-old girls," Jean said unhappily.

"Complicated isn't necessarily a bad thing," Lea said softly. "I just want you to know something."

"What?"

"You can trust me," Lea finished, her tone still gentle. "That's all. If you want to talk to someone, you're safe with me."

Was she? Jean wondered.

CHAPTER SEVEN

When Jean looked up from her desk, she saw Todd Moorman hovering in her office door. Why couldn't he just knock on the doorframe like a normal human being instead of waiting for her to notice him? She suppressed the sigh of annoyance she seemed to always feel when she saw him. "Todd. What's up?"

"Can I disturb you a minute?" he asked.

You already have, she thought. "What's going on?"

He slid into the room and braced himself with his hands on the back of her visitor's chair. She wondered how he had managed to hang up his suit coat so that the lapel was creased at an odd angle. Was he married? She couldn't remember. Glancing down she saw a thin silver band on the third finger of his left hand, so it seemed he was. Apparently his wife hadn't been able to help him figure out how to hang up his jacket properly.

"I was wondering…" His voice trailed off.

"Yes?" She heard the sharpness in her tone.

"I, uh, wondered if you have any more work for me," he managed, fiddling with the end of his tie. "The planning commission cases have really slowed down lately, I don't know if it's the economy or just the end of summer, and public works doesn't need a lot of legal advice generally and I'm kind of—"

She interrupted him, fearful that the sentence would never end. "I understand, Todd. I have a couple of things I could give you. And I do appreciate your willingness to ask."

He looked gratified. Jean picked up a file from the corner of her desk. She said, "This is a pretty straightforward legal issue from the public trustee about agricultural redemption periods. It shouldn't take you more than a couple of hours, but she needs it by the end of the week. Can you do that?"

"Oh, sure thing," he said eagerly, taking the folder.

Glancing at the pile of file folders in the corner, Jean had a sudden inspiration. "I have a bigger project for you too. The file over there is the Lambert case."

"The public works guy? He was suing us, right?"

"Yes. He died last week, killed by the burglar who's been stealing from homes in Joya. I need you to review the case and research the survivability of the lawsuit."

Jean saw the look of confusion that Todd was trying to hide and she wondered what had possessed Del Franklin to hire him. Todd seemed nice enough, but nothing about his intellect impressed her. Jean explained, "Some tort suits survive the death of the plaintiff, some don't. You need to research whether this type of suit can be continued by Lambert's estate or whether we can get it dismissed because of his death. Start with the Colorado statutes and then do whatever case law research on Westlaw you need to do about interpretation."

"Okay, got it," he said and at least he seemed eager to tackle the problem.

"You should have a couple of weeks to do it," she told him as he gathered up the folders from her chair. "If Lambert's attorney files a Motion for Substitution of Parties I'll let you know, but I'm hoping we can get a definitive answer before that happens. Get back to me if you have a question, all right?"

"Absolutely, you bet," Todd said, and gathered up the files and quickly left. Jean could not remember the last time she'd given an assignment to anyone who reacted with such enthusiasm.

Thinking about Lambert made her think of Lea and that triggered her memory of Saturday night. The party had felt mostly like a work obligation, but the dance in the moonlight with Lea had been something different, very personal.

And perhaps even more than just something private. Why had Lea asked her to dance? Perhaps it really had been just a whim, Lea's desire to dance with another woman. Or was Lea being less than honest about her motive that she wanted to be friends and nothing more?

Jean wanted to laugh at herself. She was the one being dishonest, pretending that her attraction to Lea didn't exist. And she was lying to Lea as well, which was worse. It was time, well past time, for the two of them to have a serious conversation. Lea needed to know that Jean wasn't available for any kind of relationship.

She looked longingly at her office phone with its two lines, hold and speaker buttons. It would be so much easier to have the conversation with Lea on the telephone, without having to look into her eyes or see her hands or remember how soft her hair was.

This was getting her nowhere. She couldn't call Lea to explain, so she was going to have to set up a lunch or something. She could always use their plan to reintroduce Rita to Loren as an excuse, she supposed.

* * *

"Rita Lopez," Lea repeated, replacing her napkin in her lap. "I didn't remember her, but I dug out Loren's yearbook and looked her up. Honor Society, girls choir, debate club. She was a pretty girl, at least at sixteen."

"She's the best paralegal in the office and she's still nice-looking. And by the way, research skills like yours could get you through law school," Jean responded lightly.

"There's no need to be insulting," Lea responded, giving her a crooked smile.

"You are hilarious. And here I thought all you law enforcement types were so serious."

"Stereotyping is such a bad thing. I'll have you know I was voted class clown in high school."

"Now I know you're kidding."

Lea grinned again. "Yep," she admitted.

"I'm going to go with most likely to succeed."

"Wrong this time."

"Well, come on, Sheriff, fess up. I've only got an hour for lunch."

"Oh, come on. It's casual Friday."

"That refers to my extremely relaxed wardrobe, not to my workload." Jean was wearing khakis and a cotton cardigan, as casual as she could bring herself to dress for work. "You look fine," Lea said. "Very informal and southern Colorado appropriate."

"Says a woman who wears a starched uniform to work every day."

"It makes decision making in the mornings easier. And remember," Lea gestured with her spoon, "the most important element: no pantyhose."

Jean laughed. "I'm glad you have your priorities straight." She happily tried her tomato basil soup. "So tell me. Why did you pick law enforcement instead of ranching or selling insurance or law school? Was it just that your grandfather was the sheriff?"

Touching her mouth with the napkin, Lea said thoughtfully, "It's hard to go back and separate your own desires or inclinations from the influence of the people around you. My grandfather was one of my favorite people growing up. He always seemed to be so...I don't know, calm and in control, as if there were no situation he couldn't handle. I wanted to be like that." Her mouth quirked up again and Jean realized how adorable she found that expression. "I have a strong instinct to keep people safe, I guess. I really love my job." She tasted her green chile stew and smiled. "This is good. So, your turn. Why law school?"

Jean shrugged. "I liked school and I was good at it. Being a lawyer seemed likely to make me more money than being a college professor."

Lea gave her a sharply assessing look. "Money is important to you?"

"Not per se. But getting away from my mother was very important to me when I was eighteen and money was just a tool for that."

Lea's tense shoulders relaxed slightly and Jean realized that she'd been worried that money was Jean's priority. "So that worked to get you away?" Lea asked.

"Well enough. I escaped to get away from the Texas heat and humidity and moved to California, the land of mudslides and earthquakes." She finished off her soup. "Enough about me. I thought we were here to talk about Loren."

Jean didn't really care very much what the topic was, she realized. The crush she had finally admitted she had on Lea was making the second part of the upcoming conversation between them, the explanation about Charlotte, that much more difficult to think about.

Lea said, "Yes, right. Loren and Rita. We could just do this the old-fashioned way and set them up on a blind date."

"Well, not exactly a blind date. They have met, even if it was a lot of years ago."

Lea munched on a piece of tortilla thoughtfully. "I'm really reluctant to get too clever and try to arrange a 'gee, look who's here' encounter. It feels a little manipulative to me."

Propping her chin in her hand, Jean mused, "If I ask Rita directly if she's interested in going out with Loren and she says no, that solves the problem, I guess. If she says yes, and I'm betting that she will, do we just get her number and give it to Loren to call her?"

"Seems the most direct way," Lea agreed. "If he doesn't want to, neither one of them is risking much in the way of damaged pride."

"Oh, I don't know," Jean said. "If he doesn't call her after I get her phone number, I think that might hurt her feelings a bit."

Lea looked thoughtful and Jean gazed out the front window of the downtown bistro at the people on the sidewalk. The natives were strolling, stopping to chat or go into the small shops, most wearing some variation of denim, cowboy hats and boots. The tourists, and there were always some, usually walked at a brisker pace and seemed to favor polyester and tennis shoes. At length Lea sighed. "Yep, I guess you're right. We're making this way too hard. Let's just go to lunch this weekend, the four of us, and tell everybody what's up. They can chat and mutually decide to do whatever they want to do. Or not. How's that?"

"It took forty minutes and two highly intelligent professional women to figure out that strategy?" Jean smiled. "Glad we weren't doing something really hard."

Lea, keeping her voice low but with a bantering tone, responded, "It's because it's men and women. Lesbians are so much easier to get together."

Jean laughed out loud, attracting a few curious stares from other diners.

The waitress appeared, to whisk away bowls and refill the iced tea glasses. "So what's going on with our jail death case?" Lea asked.

"We have a settlement conference set for November, the fifth I think. But the good news is that after your deposition, I got a call from plaintiff's counsel, which was, you might say, an exploratory one."

"Sending out feelers for settlement, is that what you mean?"

"Exactly. They're on their way down in the demand amount and I'm going to the board next week to nail down some settlement authority. It will probably be in the low six-figure range."

"Still seems like a lot when we weren't at fault," Lea muttered.

"It is," Jean agreed. "But it will cost us at least two hundred thousand or so to try the case, when you figure in time off for our witnesses, attorney costs, preparation for trial and expert-witness fees. It's just an economic decision, as we talked about before."

Lea sighed. "I know. Cost of doing the public business, in a way."

"Exactly."

Before Jean could determine how to introduce the subject she really had to talk about, Lea reached for the cell phone on her belt. She looked at the number, and then said apologetically, "I'm sorry, it's the office."

"I understand," Jean said, both disappointed and relieved. "You're always on call."

"This is Hawkins," Lea said into the phone. She listened intently for about a minute and then said, "What's his status?" After another pause, she said, "Okay. I'm on my way in. Tell Cruz and Hopkins I'll see them before they go in to talk to him. Yes, I'll be there in fifteen."

She punched the phone off. "Sorry, I have to go."

"Good news or bad?"

"Good, I hope." She lowered her voice carefully and continued, "My investigators finally got a tip and they located an individual at the flea market selling some stuff stolen in a couple of the Joya burglaries. We just arrested the guy we think is our burglar."

"That is good news," Jean exclaimed. "Are you going to take over the case now?"

Lea frowned at her. "I don't step in and take cases away from my people after they've done all the work. I just want to make sure we're on the road to getting a confession, especially for the murder of Fred Lambert. And we'll need to do a press release, or maybe a news conference and that's my job."

Jean was afraid she'd offended her. "Sorry, I didn't mean to—"

Lea interrupted her with a wave of a dismissive hand. "It's fine. Look, would you be willing to do me a favor? Work-related, I mean."

"Of course."

"I'll want to brief the board on the arrest but I'll need more information first. Would you see if they're willing to meet late this afternoon, say four o'clock? I know it's Friday afternoon but they really like knowing what's going on with high-profile cases like this and I don't want them to be surprised with a phone call from the press later."

"No problem," Jean said. "I'll call them myself and let Del know."

Lea stood up from the table, but hesitated. "I understand you need to tell your boss," she said, "but you're my lawyer. I want you in on the briefing too. All right?"

Jean had a warm flutter in her stomach. Don't be an idiot, she chided herself. It's just work.

"I'll be there," she promised.

* * *

The sun was still above the mountaintops when the three commissioners, two attorneys and the sheriff assembled in the commissioners' conference room. As usual the commissioners took the seats to give them the western-facing view. Del and Jean sat across from them, as befitted their lowly status as mere employees, though Jean noticed that Del managed to get the seat directly across from Carolyn Forsythe.

Lea sat at the head of the table and Jean observed how her calm presence seemed to fill a room. Lea folded her hands on the tabletop and Jean found herself gazing at her, enjoying the sight.

I have got to get a handle on this, she told herself yet again. But it would be so much easier if Lea weren't so nice. And attractive. And sexy.

Stop, stop, stop.

"Thank you for coming." Lea began the meeting. "I needed to update you on the newest developments in the case concerning the Joya burglaries and, of course, the Lambert murder, in case you received any phone calls from the press or constituents."

"We do so appreciate it, Sheriff." Carolyn oozed charm.

"Could we get on with this?" Del muttered.

Lea shot him a look that shut him up and Jean realized how much Lea actively disliked Del Franklin. We have so much in common, she thought wryly. Lea continued, "Today at around noon, two of my investigators assigned to the case executed an arrest warrant on one William Crabtree Junior, age twenty, a resident of Joya. He lives with his parents, William Senior and Nina Crabtree."

She paused a moment to see if anyone reacted to the names, then went on. "The arrest warrant was issued this morning after we received information that Crabtree was selling a video game system and sound equipment similar to items stolen in two of the Joya burglaries. We have since verified that the items were in fact stolen from the homes burglarized last month and by executing a search warrant on the Crabtree home this afternoon, we have recovered most of the stolen goods."

"Good news," Jaime Fontana said. "So he's your guy, then."

Lea looked hesitant and Jean wondered what was going on. "After being booked, Mr. Crabtree was questioned by our investigators. He declined counsel and eventually admitted to having committed the burglaries." She cleared her throat and added, "He was apparently under the mistaken impression that since he was not yet twenty-one, he could not be charged as an adult. My investigators have since corrected him and explained that he became an adult at age eighteen for purposes of the criminal statutes. In any event, he has signed a complete confession and stated that he acted alone. We certainly have no indication that he acted with anyone else. He told us the motive for the thefts was a desire to get money to move out of his parents' home."

Well, he's out of their house now, Jean thought, mulling over the irony, and he's likely to stay that way. She had finally figured out what Lea wasn't telling them as Jaime Fontana said, "He admitted to the murder too, right?"

Lea refolded her hands and looked him in the face. "No."

"No?" Del and Carolyn said almost in unison.

"He has categorically denied ever being in the Lambert house and says he had nothing to do with Lambert's murder."

Hayward Lyons said loudly, "That's the biggest load of bullshit I've ever heard! I hope you recognize a lying piece of shit when you see one, Sheriff!"

"Ward, language," Carolyn murmured.

"I'm sure the sheriff has heard worse language," Lyons snarled. "I'm sure the sheriff has *used* worse language, in fact."

Lea ignored the comment. "There are a couple of complicating factors. First, Crabtree has an alibi of sorts for the Lambert murder. He was with some friends that evening and didn't get home until after midnight."

"Friends!" Lyons snorted. "People who would lie to cover up for him, no doubt."

"It's always possible," Lea said in a tone that indicated she was doubtful. "We'll follow up of course on the witnesses he mentioned. He told us they were playing some video games and that he was with them from six o'clock on. If we can verify his alibi, it appears he may not have committed the Lambert murder."

Jean did a quick survey of the faces at the table. Hayward and Del looked deeply skeptical, Carolyn looked shocked and Jaime had the expression of a man who couldn't believe what he was hearing.

"I don't understand," Jaime said at length. "I thought you were sure that the same man, the burglar, killed Lambert."

"At the time, it was a reasonable theory," Lea said coolly, "but there were some inconsistencies that made it less than a certainty."

"This is still bullshit," Lyons said decisively. "He did it and you know he did it. He's just afraid to confess to a murder, that's all."

Lea turned to him. "That may be true. But as I said, he may have an alibi. In addition, the Lambert break-in wasn't exactly the same MO as the others and, most importantly, we haven't found anything to tie Crabtree to the Lambert murder. No physical traces were left behind that we can tie to Crabtree and there was nothing at the Crabtree house that links him to the Lambert murder. And of course we haven't found the gun."

Across the table, Jean could hear Hayward Lyons grinding his teeth. Beside him, Carolyn said, "Oh, Ward, come on now. We know you campaigned on a law and order platform and all that, but really. You have to let the investigators do their jobs." She flashed a smile at Lea and added, "Ward would have made an excellent hanging judge, I'm sure."

Del said, "Well frankly, I agree with Hayward. I assume you'll work to get this resolved as soon as possible, Sheriff."

Jean watched both Carolyn and Ward glance at Del, but she couldn't read either expression. At length, Ward muttered, "You're right, of course, Carolyn. We trust you to wrap this up correctly, Sheriff Hawkins, to see that justice is done."

Fixing Del with a glare that would have caused Jean to cower if it had been aimed at her, Lea responded, "Don't worry. We will make an arrest for this murder. We're starting from scratch, investigating anyone else who had a motive to kill Fred Lambert."

"You think it was someone he knew?" Carolyn exclaimed.

"The majority of murder victims know their killers," Lea answered. "If Crabtree did it, we'll make every effort to find enough proof to go to the district attorney and charge Crabtree with the murder. If we clear him, we'll find out who did fire the gun. Any questions?"

Her tone wasn't particularly inviting and Jean wasn't surprised when no one spoke.

Lea rose. She said briskly, "I'll keep you updated as the investigation progresses. In the meantime, I'd appreciate it if you referred any questions from the newspaper or television stations to me directly. I'm preparing a press release for this evening's broadcast deadlines and doing a stand-up interview in…" she consulted her watch, "fifteen minutes. Thank you for coming in on a Friday afternoon."

She left without a backward glance. The set of her shoulders looked angry and Jean couldn't tell if Lea was more furious at the board or at the suspect. Either way, Jean was glad she wasn't the object of her wrath.

On her way back to her office, Jean remembered that she still hadn't talked to Lea about their relationship. She suspected that with the investigation now on the front burner, it would be a while before she and Lea would have another relaxed lunch conversation.

* * *

To avoid going to the gym on Saturday morning, Jean was forced to clean her entire condo, from vacuuming to dusting to cleaning the toilet. She made a list of things she needed to get for the house: bedroom rug, extra light bulbs, a large laundry basket.

When the workout could be delayed no longer, she reluctantly put on her sweats and a T-shirt with a faded University of Texas Longhorns logo. Once on the treadmill she thought, as she often did, that the treadmill used to be a punishment for prisoners sentenced to hard labor in nineteenth-century England. And now we pay good money for the privilege. She shook her head with a small smile.

She finished her forty minutes and eyed the free weights, talking herself out of further exertion. She wondered if Lea worked out in her home gym every morning or if, like herself, she just managed three or four times a week. Jean didn't think she could bear to have workout equipment at home, always standing mutely, waiting for her and making her feel guilty.

And there she was thinking about Lea Hawkins again. There were probably fewer than a dozen single gay women in the entire county and she had to have the sexiest lesbian available as a client. Just remembering Lea's long, strong fingers or her crooked smile was giving Jean a burning feeling under her skin, a feeling so long absent she could scarcely remember what it felt like. She knew it was desire, naked and compelling, and she didn't know what to do with it.

She stripped off her clothes as soon as she walked in the door and started the shower. She ought to take a cold shower, she supposed, but she turned the water steamy hot and stepped into the cascade of warmth. The shower prickled on her skin, washing over her shoulders and down her back. She leaned forward against the tiles, cold against the palm of one hand as she slid her other hand between her legs.

She tried very hard not to think about Lea, her mouth or her fingers, but she could dream of nothing else, no one else. She climaxed silently, pressing her forehead into the cool tile and seeing only Lea's face before her.

CHAPTER EIGHT

Rita Lopez toyed with the ends of her silverware, still tightly rolled up in her napkin.

"Are you nervous?" Jean asked gently.

"No," Rita answered quickly. "Yes, I guess. A little. It's been a long time since I've been on a date."

After days of delicate negotiation, dinner had been substituted for lunch and Lea had suggested Carelli's, which despite the name was a steakhouse rather than an Italian restaurant. Carelli's was close to the nicest place in town and Jean wondered at the choice. It made the get-together seem more formal than she would have thought advisable.

Rita had certainly dressed for the evening. She was wearing a bright red wrap dress and a matching set of jet-black necklace and earrings.

"Don't worry, you look great," Jean reassured her. "And it can't be that long since you've been on a date, I bet."

Rita lowered her head a little. "You'd be wrong," she said softly. "I got married right out of high school, had a baby when

I was nineteen. He wanted more children right away but I wanted to go to community college. We fought all the time and at twenty-one I was divorced and on my own with Jay." She looked up at Jean and smiled a little. "His name is Jesús, but he likes to go by Jay. He's thirteen going on thirty. Man of the house, you know. Not a lot of guys want to date a woman with a teenaged son already."

Jean looked up to see Lea and Loren coming across the dining room floor. Loren was propelling himself in his wheelchair, with Lea following behind. Lea was wearing her usual off-duty attire of jeans and western-style shirt, but Loren had clearly dressed up for the evening. He was wearing a white silk shirt with the cowboy yoke outlined in black piping and a handsome black onyx bolo tie. His brushed-felt black cowboy hat was in his lap and his dark eyes were alight with pleasure.

"Hi," he said, wheeling up to the table where Jean had asked the hostess to remove one of the chairs for him. "Jean, it's nice to see you again."

Jean rose and kissed him on the cheek. He was freshly shaven and smelled faintly of soap. "Good to see you too, handsome," she said. "You will behave this evening, won't you?"

Loren laughed then turned to Rita. "Hi," he said again, warmth in his voice.

"Hello," she said shyly. "I'm sure you don't remember me."

"I do actually, Rita." He grinned. "You sang the national anthem before one of the football games my senior year, didn't you?"

She nodded shyly. They fell into conversation immediately, reminiscing about high school. Lea sat down next to Jean, leaned in and murmured, "So far, so good."

Jean turned her head and caught a faint scent of something fresh that was reminiscent of the desert: sage, perhaps. God, Lea even smelled good to her. She swallowed and replied, "Let's keep our fingers crossed. How have you been?"

"Fine, except for the stinking mess that is the Lambert murder investigation."

"Field full of cow patties, is it?" Jean asked.

"I'll have you know those are called meadow muffins, you tenderfoot."

Jean laughed. Had Charlotte ever made her laugh this much? She couldn't remember.

"What's wrong with the investigation?" she asked. "Or can't you tell me?"

Lea glanced at Loren and Rita, still deep into their conversation. "I thought I could tell you anything, Counselor."

Jean raised her hand, palm outward. "Girl Scout's honor."

"You don't look like the Girl Scout type to me, but I'll take a chance. Crabtree's alibi checked out. He continues to swear he knows nothing about Lambert's murder and we have nothing to tie him to the shooting. My investigators are now convinced he's not guilty of the murder and they're usually very skeptical people. This time I agree with them. Which puts us back at square one. Lambert's wife was in full view of her bridge club all evening, he got along with his neighbors, he apparently didn't have much money or insurance to speak of and no known enemies. Worked for county road and bridge twenty-two years."

"Until he got fired," Jean mused.

Lea looked at her sharply. "That's right, you told me about that. What have you found out about the suit?"

Jean shook her head. "I assigned the research project to one of the assistants and I haven't had a chance to talk about it with him."

"Follow up, will you? There's probably nothing in it, but we need something to go on. Presumably if he was angry enough to sue, there was some animosity, on his part at least."

Jean looked thoughtful. "I know he was claiming he was wrongfully terminated by the county. I wonder if one of his supervisors had it in for him."

"It's not much of a motive, but I've seen less." Lea glanced again at Loren and Rita, who had moved on to rodeo as a topic. "Do you think we'll be getting dinner any time this evening?"

"We should be pleased it's going so well," Jean said with a hint of smugness.

"Oh, I am." Lea gave her an enigmatic smile. "I'm a romantic at heart."

Jean felt her own heart thud against her breastbone. "Are you?"

"Yes. I keep it well hidden except for my closest friends." Lea gave her the half smile and Jean thought her beating heart must be visible beneath her blouse. It might have been a very long time, but Jean knew flirting when she heard it.

"What am I going to do?" Jean murmured.

"What?" Lea asked.

"I said, what am I going to do for dinner? Ah, have for dinner, I mean. What are you having?"

Lea opened a menu. "If you like steak, I can recommend anything on the menu. I usually get the New York strip."

"You are such a carnivore," Jean teased.

"Guilty, Counselor."

Jean looked at the menu, trying to decide what to do about dinner and what to do about her life.

Eventually Loren and Rita let them into the conversation and they enjoyed their dinner and evening. By the time after-dinner coffee was served, Loren had made plans to go to Jay's soccer game the next day. Lea was smiling happily at everyone, her brother, Rita and especially Jean. Relieved that their plan seemed to be going well, Jean enjoyed her meal. The brussels sprouts were a little underdone and bitter, but her steak was fine. At least all those years living with a chef had given her some appreciation for a well-cooked meal.

Rita walked toward the parking lot beside Loren as he wheeled his way out, with Jean and Lea trailing behind. Near the door, Lea stopped Jean with a hand on her arm.

"Would you like to go riding tomorrow?" Lea asked. "It's been a while since I've been and being on a horse always relaxes me. This week has been hellish. Or don't you ride?"

"I used to when I was at school," Jean admitted. "It's been a few years. We're not doing anything too difficult, I hope."

"No, just an easy ride to one of my favorite places on my parents' ranch. Later in the afternoon if that's okay."

Jean realized that she'd apparently agreed to go without actually saying so. Maybe it was just as well, she sighed inwardly. Alone in the middle of the desert was probably the best place to finally have the conversation about Charlotte.

* * *

Jean got out of her car and managed to get the door closed just as the dogs rounded the corner of the house on a dead run. This time she waited until they reached her and then said, "Good dogs. Doc, Wyatt, sit."

The dogs went down, tails still wagging. Jean petted them both thoroughly until they were dancing and wiggling in pleasure.

"Okay, you two," Jean said and they bounced away, leading her back to the barn. She went in to find Lea slipping a bridle onto a beautiful brown-and-white paint horse. Tied securely nearby was a second smaller horse, a dapple gray, already saddled and bridled.

"Hi," Jean said. "I see I timed it perfectly, letting you do all the work and showing up just in time for the fun stuff."

"Good job," Lea said dryly.

Both horses received a greeting from Jean, who enjoyed the silky soft feel of the horses' muzzles. "I brought presents," Jean said. "Are they allowed?"

Lea tried to look stern. "Not sugar, I hope?"

"No, apples, a healthy snack. I like to make friends with my mount before the ride."

"Very wise. Please go ahead, bribe your horse."

Jean produced the apples, carefully doling out one per horse, offering them flat on her palms to prevent a mistakenly chewed finger. As the horses crunched happily, Lea petted the paint horse. She said, "This is Horatio, one of my father's best stallions."

Jean looked him over. She said cautiously, "I'm not riding him, I hope."

"Nope. He and I are working on some of his obedience issues, but he's going to be a good boy today, aren't you? You're on Amelia there."

"She's a lovely mare, but she's not a paint," Jean observed, stroking the gray-flecked coat.

Lea smiled. "She's my horse. Gentle, and a sure-footed mount. You'll like her."

"Your horse? She lives here?"

"Yep. She gets plenty of exercise this way and I get to ride whenever I have a chance. I also pay for her board, which helps out my parents in slow months. You ready?"

They mounted. "I have some water in the canteens so be sure to drink as we go," Lea said as they rode out. "It's a dry climate."

"So everyone keeps telling me," Jean remarked. "I don't seem to be able to keep enough hand lotion in the house."

There were stratocumulus clouds thick above the line of the mountain range before them. As they rode in a mostly westerly direction, Jean spent a few minutes adjusting to using her riding muscles again, but Amelia was as easy a ride as Lea had promised. Soon Jean was able to relax and enjoy the scenery.

"What are those mountains called?" she asked after a while. "I mean, I know they're the Rockies, but does that range have a specific name?"

"They're called the Wet Mountains. Because of the geography they get more than their share of moisture, usually in the form of winter snow. The tallest one, there? That's Greenhorn Mountain, a little over twelve thousand feet." She pointed south to a pair of mountains that seemed to stand a little apart from the rest of the range. "Those two are actually the easternmost Rockies in the entire range. The local Indian tribe called them 'The Breasts of the World.'"

Jean admired the mountains for a moment then shifted around in her saddle to glance over her shoulder. "And that's Pike's Peak to the north, right?"

"Yep. It's much taller, more than fourteen thousand feet. It's the only Colorado fourteener where you can drive to the top. The rest of them require you to hike."

Jean smiled. "No, thank you very much. I think I'll stick with Amelia. She's great, by the way."

"I'm glad you two are getting along. She's named after Amelia Earhart, one of my childhood heroes."

Jean cocked her head. "You know, I didn't think of it before, but you look a lot like pictures I've seen of her."

"Thank you kindly, ma'am."

If Lea was following some path along the sandy soil, Jean couldn't discern it. They seemed to be randomly picking their way through the scrubby green trees, low bushes and rocks, avoiding the dry arroyos as they went.

"Did you ever wonder what you'd have done if you'd lived a hundred years ago?" Jean asked. "I can see you as a barnstormer, myself."

"Oh, I don't think so." Lea laughed. "I like my feet on the ground, thanks. Too bad I couldn't have been a US marshal in the days of the wild, wild West. I would love to spend a lot less time on budget reports and applying for federal grants and a lot more time going after the bad guys."

Jean mused, "I can see that too. Six gun strapped to your hip, strolling down the wooden sidewalks, tipping your hat to all the ladies."

"Oh, I'm sure that would have gone over well," Lea said dryly.

"Don't be so literal." Jean twitched the reins to guide Amelia around a big rock. "Come on now. Are you hanging out at the Long Branch Saloon, wooing the local Miss Kitty? Of maybe you'd rather pay court to some nice widowed shopkeeper. Does calico do anything for you?"

Jean was enjoying the light-hearted conversation, but Lea said suddenly, "You mean like the blouse you wore to the Harvest Moon Party?"

Jean was suddenly having trouble swallowing and she groped for the canteen hung on her saddle horn. "Lea—"

But Lea interrupted her with, "I'm thinking I'm going after the brave woman rancher trying to make a go of it on her own land."

"Oh." Jean managed to recover. "So now we're casting Barbara Stanwyck in *The Big Valley*."

"Hmm." Lea thought it over. "Maybe. Though there was a lot of testosterone on the ranch with all those hunky sons hanging around. Even better, how about the marshal courts the local schoolmarm? Those delicate little glasses and all."

There wasn't enough water in the canteen for her to deal with Lea flirting with her like this. Jean swallowed and then ventured, "You're going for an early twentieth-century version of geek girl?"

"Pretty sure 'geek' wasn't part of the vocabulary then," Lea said. "What would you call an educated, intelligent woman a hundred years ago?"

"A bluestocking," Jean answered.

"Really?"

"Yes. It originally was a group of well-educated women in the eighteenth century, I think."

"The things you know, Counselor." Lea smiled. "*The Marshal and the Bluestocking*. I'm not sure that's really a compelling title."

Jean found a laugh. "*The Marshal and the Schoolmarm* doesn't exactly sing, either."

Lea led them up a little rise that seemed to grow steeper. She guided her horse in front of Jean. "It's kind of single file through here. Don't worry, Amelia knows the way."

When they completed the climb up the hill, Lea dropped Horatio back to ride beside her again. "*The Marshal and the Shopkeeper* isn't going to cut it. I think we'd better go back to the brave woman rancher scenario."

"Yes, we need a snappier title for our little lesbian western," Jean said. "Perhaps a place name like *The High Chaparral*." She glanced up at the mountains again. "Maybe *Greenhorn Ranch*?"

"Nope, sounds too much like a dude ranch. And I definitely do not recommend using Pike's Peak or Breasts of the World in any way, shape or form."

Jean started laughing. "I guess you won't let me use some variation on the Wet Mountains, then."

"Hell no!" Lea said forcefully.

Jean considered the problem. "How about *Don't Fence Me In?*"

Lea considered it thoughtfully. "Not bad, but—wait, I think I've got it."

"Don't keep me in suspense."

"I'm thinking, *Meanwhile, Back at the Ranch*."

They were both laughing now. Jean was amused by Lea and attracted to her in the same moment.

There was a crest at the top of a little mesa wide enough for both horses to stand side by side. Above them, a solitary hawk circled, wings spread wide, coasting on a thermal as it scanned the ground for a rabbit or prairie chicken. Below them the sandy landscape, dotted with dark green, spread expansively to the far away blue-gray hills. Lea had timed the ride so that the sun was beginning to set, bleeding from rose to peach to orange, the color in the clouds changing every few moments.

"Oh, my God," Jean said.

"My favorite spot for sunset viewing," Lea said. "I was hoping it would be particularly nice this evening with the right amount of clouds. I'm glad you like it."

They sat quietly in their saddles. The horses waited patiently, shifting occasionally from foot to foot. The sunset before them was setting the clouds aflame with deep orange and scarlet red, as if the clouds were burning with a fire from within. The sky behind the clouds was a light blue and the contrast with the dark blue mountains made the colors bright as a tropical ocean. Jean couldn't keep her eyes from the spectacle. It was like watching a fireworks display exploding in slow motion, a dozen different shades of the same color blending slowly. The oranges and reds eased into purples and lavenders as they watched.

The colors began to darken, the sky turning to a deeper blue. Finally Jean said the only thing she could say.

"It's so beautiful," she said softly.

Lea eased Horatio into a wide circle around the top of the mesa until she brought him next to Jean and Amelia again, this time with the horses nose to tail. Lea pulled up until she faced Jean, their knees touching.

"It is beautiful," Lea said, her voice low. "And so are you."

She put her hand on Jean's saddle horn to keep them close. Lea waited a moment, to give her time to protest. But Jean wanted nothing else.

Lea leaned in toward her. Jean didn't wait for the kiss—she met Lea halfway there. Warm and smooth, Lea's mouth against hers heated her down to her core. Jean had never felt so much from a single kiss. Lea broke their contact and sat back a little to look into Jean's eyes. Jean didn't know what Lea was looking for and at that moment she didn't care. All she wanted was for Lea to kiss her again.

Whatever Lea read in her face was enough and Jean welcomed another kiss, longer and deeper this time. When they finally stopped, Lea's hand came up and gently caressed Jean's cheek with the backs of her fingers.

Jean couldn't remember what she wanted to tell Lea, why she couldn't pursue a relationship with her or anything else, even where she was. She could barely remember her own name while Lea was touching her.

Lea said quietly, "We should get back before it gets any darker. Follow me down, okay?"

Clinging to Amelia's back as they descended the little hill, Jean felt almost dizzy. The air at dusk had cooled the desert, but she realized that she wasn't cold anymore. Lea's kisses had warmed her from the inside out and set her skin alive with electricity.

The white fence of the corral shimmered ahead of them in the gathering darkness as they rode in. A silent Jean helped Lea unsaddle the horses. Lea tossed Jean a curry comb and Jean brushed Amelia down, welcoming the mundane routine of the task to calm her turbulent emotions.

When the horses were safely back in their stalls, Jean said, "I think we both need something to drink."

"Yep. I'll go inside and grab some water."

"Aren't your parents home?"

"No, they're at some church function tonight and Loren is apparently still out with your friend Rita. Meet you on the porch?"

Jean found a comfortable seat near the front door and watched the last streaks of reflected pink fade from the clouds in the east. Wyatt and Doc came out to join her, each dog taking a spot on either side of the padded bench. She dropped her hand down to pet Wyatt's floppy ears and he leaned his head against the bench in happiness.

Lea emerged from the house, a tall glass with ice in each hand. "There was lemonade in the fridge, so I made an executive decision. Okay with you?"

"Wonderful," Jean said, taking a glass from her.

They sat in the quiet for a while, enjoying the lemonade and petting the happy dogs. The stars began to appear as pinpricks of sharp light in the darkening sky. The moon, waning down to a half circle, hung low over the horizon.

Jean asked, "Why did you kiss me?"

She heard the clink of ice against glass as Lea set it down on the porch. Lea answered, "It's not hard to figure out, Jean. I like you. You make me laugh. I like being with you, I'm attracted to you and I wanted to kiss you. Was that all right?"

Jean sighed. "Lea, I like you too. But we can't have a relationship other than friendship, so I don't think we should act as if we could."

Lea was silent for a long time before she said, "You're not interested."

"I didn't say that. I said we shouldn't become involved."

Turning toward her, Lea said, "Does that mean you are interested?"

"You're not listening to me," Jean snapped at her in irritation. "It's irrelevant whether I am or not. We can't date and that's all there is."

"Are you going to tell me why?"

"First and foremost, you're my client. Lawyers can't date clients, end of discussion."

"I'm willing to assume you're right about that," Lea answered, "but we both know there are ways around that."

Jean frowned. "What are you talking about?"

"I'll go to your boss and ask for another attorney to be assigned to the sheriff's office."

"If you do that, you'll have to give him some explanation."

"Well, here's a radical thought," Lea remarked dryly. "I could tell him the truth."

"You're really willing to come out to Del Franklin?" Jean asked in astonishment.

"I am if that's what I need to do to go out with you."

Jean shook her head. "I don't want you to have to do that. Even if we could have a relationship, I—I can't."

"You can't," Lea repeated stoically. "I ask again: are you going to tell me why?"

Jean sighed. "Because of Charlotte."

"Charlotte is...?"

"Oh, sorry. Charlotte was my partner."

"Ah. The chef, right. She's the reason? How long has it been since she left?"

"Not quite two years."

"You're still in love with her," Lea said flatly and Jean could hear the ache behind her voice.

"What?" Jean was astonished.

"You told me that she left you. You haven't gotten over her, that's why you don't feel as if you want to date anyone else. You still love her."

Jean couldn't decide whether to laugh or cry. "No, that's not it."

"You don't still love her?"

"It wouldn't matter if I did or not," Jean said bitterly. "She's dead."

She couldn't see Lea's face very clearly, but she could feel Lea's astonishment even in the darkness. "Oh, God, Jean, I had no idea. I'm so sorry."

Shaking her head, Jean said, "Don't apologize. You didn't know. I just usually tell people she left me because it's easier. No explanations needed." She drank the rest of her lemonade, finding the last dregs sour in her mouth.

"How did she die?" Lea asked gently. "Natural causes? Or was there an accident?"

"Neither one, really," Jean considered. "There was nothing natural about it and it was quite intentional, so it hardly qualifies as an accident."

It was still hard to say the word so she let Lea put it together herself. Finally Lea said, "She committed suicide."

"Yes," Jean was able to release a long breath.

"Tell me about it," Lea said simply.

Jean had never really told anyone, she realized. Only her best friend back in Texas knew it all because she'd lived through it with Jean long distance. Her other friends and Charlotte's knew enough of the story not to need any explanations and the rest of it was none of their business. Her family didn't care and her new friends didn't know to ask. "When I met her, she was enthusiastic, energetic, entertaining. She was on top of the world, there was nothing she couldn't do, or wouldn't try. She was almost reckless, but so very charming. Then, a few months after we moved in together, she fell into a depression that seemed to last a long time. She didn't talk and she couldn't sleep. She could barely drag herself to work. It was awful. I tried to help her and eventually she regained her energy. Incredibly, we went through the same pattern for three years before I finally figured out she had a mood disorder."

"It's hard to see when you're so close to it," Lea said softly.

Jean shook her head. "She was practically a textbook case of bipolar disorder, what they used to call manic-depression. I thought I should have seen it sooner. But I didn't. I kept thinking there was something happening to her at work, or something I was doing or not doing that would trigger the mood swings."

"You know it wasn't your fault, right?"

Jean gave her a sad little smile. "That would depend on who you ask. Her psychologists—and she had several over the years—told me that regularly. Charlotte had a different opinion. It was a lot easier for her to blame me than acknowledge that she had a mental illness of any kind."

"God, Jean. That must have been so hard for you."

"It was. It was worse for her. The doctors would put her on meds, the drugs would help, then she'd go off them again, convinced she didn't need them, sure she was fine. We'd have to get through whatever mood she was in, find a new shrink and start over again. And again."

Lea finally said, "And then she killed herself."

Jean dropped her head into her hands. "I told her I was going to leave her if she didn't stay on her medications and focus on getting better. I told her I loved her and I knew how hard it was, but we needed to be together without always having to fight whatever phase of the illness she was in. I went to work, I came home and I found her. She was in our bed. She'd slashed her wrists and there was so much blood—"

Jean broke down and the next moment she felt Lea's arms around her. She let the tears come, not that she could have stopped them. She'd cried a lot of tears for Char, but after a time she realized that on this evening, her tears were really for herself, for the pain and loneliness—and the guilt—she'd had since that night.

To her relief, Lea didn't try to tell her it would be all right or tell her to stop crying, as other friends had done. Lea just held on while Jean sobbed against her shoulder, Lea stroking her hair gently but doing nothing more than just being present. When Jean's weeping began to subside, Lea produced tissue for her to wipe her eyes.

"I'm sorry," Jean said. "I really didn't see that coming. It's been a long time ago now."

"There's no timeline for how to recover from things like this," Lea said. "Everyone is different, every situation is different. You never have to apologize to me for being sad."

"She left me a note," Jean added abruptly, in a hurry suddenly to finish the story. "She was very clear that her death was my fault, that if I'd been a better partner everything would have been all right." She dabbed at her eyes again with the tissue. "Her most recent psychologist thought she didn't really intend to die, that the suicide was a gesture and the note was a dramatic attempt to keep me from carrying out my threat to leave her if she didn't get treatment. I don't know if that's true. I didn't get home later than usual that evening. Maybe her therapist was right, she didn't intend to be successful and she just misjudged how fast she would bleed out. Or maybe she really wanted to die. I'll never know."

Somewhere far away a coyote yipped and then several others joined in a group howling. Wyatt lifted his head and Jean heard a small growl before Lea said, "Wyatt, it's okay. Good dog."

He settled down and Jean reached down to fondle his ears again. Jean wondered what Lea might be thinking. Anyone hearing the whole story would have to have doubts about how much blame Jean should bear for the end of the relationship. God knew Charlotte's parents blamed her for their daughter's death and a couple of their mutual friends had grave reservations about her degree of fault. Lea, who didn't know her half so well, must be suffering from the same misgivings.

Lea would now withdraw from her, backing away from a relationship with a woman whose love was so toxic her lover preferred death to living with her. She'd known it would happen once she told Lea the truth about Charlotte's death, but part of her still mourned the loss. Lea had come to mean more to her than she had suspected another woman ever could.

Better to stop it now, she told herself sternly, before it goes any further.

The sky had darkened to a blue one shade lighter than black, the moon risen to a shiny silver cup above them. A lyric from a song came into her mind, something about the moon being a harsh mistress. She shuddered.

"Are you cold?" Lea asked beside her.

"Not really. Just sad."

"I understand."

"Do you?" Jean asked. "I'm not sure I can explain to you why I believe I can't be with you—or with anybody. It scares the hell out of me just to think about it. I'm a wreck, barely able to hold it together during the day. I've had nightmares about Charlotte. Sometimes I can't concentrate. I'm afraid I don't have anything to give you. I wanted you to know that's it not about you, not at all. I like you, I really do. I just need for you respect what's going on with me right now and not push me."

Lea leaned back and stretched her legs out before her, crossing her boots at the ankles. The posture looked relaxed, but to Jean it seemed that she was tense and drawn, like a lasso thrown tightly around a cow's neck.

Lea spoke, her voice very soft. "Up on the mesa tonight, I thought you were hoping I would kiss you and you seemed to want it as much as I did. You have a lot of your life left to live, Jean. Are you so sure you're going to have to be alone the rest of your life? Or are you telling me it's just too soon?"

Jean spread her hands helplessly. "I don't know. Maybe it is too soon though it seems like it's been a long time. Or maybe my heart is just too damaged to try again."

"Is it?"

"Stop asking me questions! I don't know what else to tell you. And why the hell are you even still interested anyway? I'm not long-term relationship material. Isn't it pretty clear?"

"Not to me," Lea said gently. "What I see is that you tried everything to honor your commitment to your partner even when it was hard to do. What could be a better blueprint for a long-term relationship than that?"

Jean stood up abruptly. "Lea, stop it. I'm not available right now. End of story. Thank you for a nice evening. And don't worry, I can find my way home."

She walked across the yard, half expecting Lea to call her back or try to catch up with her. But as she drove away, she could still see Lea in shadow on the porch, surrounded by the two dogs, a still figure in the moonlight.

CHAPTER NINE

The first person Jean saw when she got to the office Monday morning was Rita Lopez. She was sitting at her desk, typing and smiling.

"Good weekend?" Jean stopped by.

"Oh!" Rita exclaimed. "Ms. McAllister, how will I ever be able to thank you?"

"You can start by calling me Jean, remember? So yesterday's soccer game went well?"

Smiling shyly, Rita said, "Well, Jay's team did score a goal, though the other team scored three, so it wasn't a victorious day, if that's what you mean."

"That's not really what I meant and I think you know it."

"Loren did come to the game and he was great. Just great. He was so nice to Jay and Jay seemed to like him too. Though Jay is kind of shy, Loren was joking around with him. I'd sort of forgotten how funny he was."

Jean said, "So, I know it's none of my business, but are you seeing him again?"

Rita blushed a little, but answered, "Yes. Thursday night. Pizza, he said, because he wanted me to bring Jay. Isn't he nice?"

I'm glad romance is going well for someone, Jean thought. "That's fantastic," she said to Rita. "I'm so pleased for you."

Looking up at her, Rita said, "It wouldn't have even started if not for you. And Sheriff Hawkins, of course. I'm really grateful to both of you."

Jean said, "You know what? You don't need to be grateful. Just try to be happy. It's hard to do, but Loren deserves a shot at it. And so do you."

"Thanks. I mean it." Rita hesitated, then said, "Are you all right? You look tired."

Jean's opinion was that she looked less tired and more like she'd been dragged behind a truck all night, but she said, "I'll be fine. Just didn't sleep well, that's all."

She dumped her briefcase next to her desk and took off her jacket. As usual, work files had reproduced on her desk over the weekend, producing offspring that covered every inch of the desktop. Sighing, Jean powered up her computer and began to go through her voice mail.

No nightmares with Charlotte had taunted her the night before for the simple reason that she hadn't been able to sleep at all. She continued to go over and over her conversation with Lea, wondering if she'd said the right things, said too much or too little. When she was exhausted from rehashing what they had said to each other, she replayed the kiss instead.

Had Charlotte ever made her feel like that? She must have once, Jean assumed. In her memory though, her time with Charlotte was either exhilarating, like riding a roller coaster without a brake, or painfully wrenching. She couldn't remember this feeling of searing desire, physical attraction melded with friendship. Charlotte had been many things to her: lover, opponent, housemate, but never, that Jean could recall, had they ever really been friends.

Everything about Lea attracted her: her mind, her sense of humor, her body. *Why am I so reluctant to believe that we could have a relationship?*

It had taken her all night to find the answer—or rather, to admit what she had suspected all along.

She hadn't forgiven herself for what happened to Charlotte. Some part of her believed Charlotte's note was true, that if she'd been a better partner she could somehow have prevented Charlotte's death. Jean didn't deserve to be happy, to have someone as wonderful as Lea in her life. Her mind knew she was wrong, but her heart wouldn't free her from her guilt.

What am going to do?

There was no answer waiting for her. Restlessly, she rose from her desk and walked down the hall. Franklin was meeting with the board in their weekly meeting already, not that she particularly wanted to talk to him anyway. She remembered that she'd promised Lea to follow up on the Lambert case file, so she went down to Todd Moorman's office, located on the less desirable east side of the building. Her promise to Lea was work-related, so she didn't feel as if she was weakening in her resolve to not to pursue the relationship just by checking on the status of the file.

She rapped on Todd's door and when he looked up, she said, "Sorry to interrupt you. I wondered if you wanted to discuss the projects I gave you."

"Oh, um, yes. I, ah, sent the memo to the public trustee on Friday about the redemption period."

"Yes, I saw the copy you sent me. The memo was fine, just a little long. Most elected officials understand legal opinions better if you can keep your memos to one page. That's not always possible, of course, but in this case you didn't need to include the case law discussions. Lay people usually don't care about court interpretations anyway. Just cite the statute and answer the question." She wondered if no one had ever given him any guidance on his work before.

"Okay. Yes, I see. Um, thanks."

Jean came around to sit in his visitor's chair and glanced at the framed picture on the edge of his desk. She leaned forward to it and asked, "May I?"

"Yes, of course."

She picked it up and saw a studio portrait of Todd and a young blond woman in front of a fake-looking outdoor background. Todd looked to be a decade or so younger, just out of college.

"Your wife?" Jean asked.

"Yes, that's Sandra," he said.

She tried to hear a hint of pride, or love, or any other emotion in his voice, but all she got was a sad wistfulness. She didn't want to pursue it, so she replaced the photograph. "Tell me about your research on the Lambert case."

He shuffled papers on his desktop, not to check his notes but just to give his hands something to do. "Um, yeah. Well. I read the survivorship statute and it looks like he—I mean, his heirs or estate or whatever—can pursue the suit against the county."

Jean had little patience for his lack of precision. "So the suit survives his death," she summarized.

"Ah, yes."

Good thing I rescued the file from the shredder, she congratulated herself. "And your assessment of the suit?"

"What?" He looked startled.

Jean counted to a silent ten then continued, "The discovery has been completed, correct? So you should have some idea after reviewing the file of the likelihood of success. Is his cause of action valid? Does the county have a valid defense?"

"I, er, I'm not really sure."

She counted to twenty this time then said, "Did you read the entire file?"

"Um, yeah, well, most of it. But I wasn't really looking at, you know, the elements of the suit itself."

Jean wondered how long she would have to wait if she decided she needed to talk to Del and tell him that Todd just might have to go. She'd need to work with him on other projects, but she seriously wondered whether he was ever going to meet her standards. She was a firm believer that government attorneys should actually be better than those in private practice, since citizens were depending on them to get it right. Few of her colleagues agreed with her, but she wasn't prepared to lower her standards for anyone else's opinion.

To Todd she said, "I want you to go through everything again and give me a complete assessment about how you believe the suit should proceed. Settlement evaluation, percentages of success at trial, amount Lambert's estate is likely to recover. End of the week, all right?" He asked for work, he was going to get it.

She watched him swallow hard above his badly knotted tie. Her hands were itching with the desire to take it off and teach him how to tie a simple Windsor knot.

"Um, yes," he answered. "I mean, I'll get it done."

Remembering her mission for Lea, Jean continued. "Good. In your review of the file, reading the depositions, did you get any sense of animosity toward Lambert from any of our witnesses? His supervisor, perhaps?"

"I...no, not really," Todd responded.

"Look for that too," Jean directed him, rising from her chair. "And get back to me as soon as you can on that."

She left without rolling her eyes. She wasn't completely convinced he was hopeless but she was certainly beginning to have her doubts.

Rita buzzed her just before the end of the day. To keep her eyes on her computer screen, Jean reached over and punched the speaker button on her phone. "Yes?"

"Call for you on line two," Rita said. "He said he didn't have your direct line and that it was personal."

Jean muttered, "I seriously doubt I have anything personal to discuss with an unknown man."

"He said his name was Ron Kraft."

A cold fear seized her throat. Ron was her stepfather. She said, "Thanks, Rita, I've got it." She punched off the speaker and picked up the receiver.

"Jean, I'm so sorry to bother you," and she knew from the tone of his voice that the news was bad. It could only be about her mother and his next words confirmed it. "Edie had a stroke. She's at Baptist Medical Center."

"How bad is it?" she managed to ask.

"Pretty bad. They're not sure. She seems paralyzed on one side and isn't talking but she's conscious, at least some of the time. I came home from golf and found her on the living room floor. Oh, God, Jean, if I'd been here…" His voice trailed off.

"Don't," Jean said sharply. "It wouldn't have made any difference. Look, I'll call and see when I can get a flight out and be there as soon as I can."

"You don't have to," he said tentatively and she knew how badly he wanted her to come. Her mother might or might not care but Ron did and he'd been as kind to her as he was able to be.

"I'll be there, Ron," she said firmly. After glancing at the clock, she added, "I don't know if I can get a flight out to Dallas tonight or not, but I'll be there this evening or in the morning. I'll call you when I know for sure. Have you called Bobby?"

He made a noise. "Yes. He's got something he couldn't get out of tonight but he said he'll be driving up tomorrow. Maybe he could pick you up at the airport."

Jean tried not to laugh. Her brother would be more likely to drive her to purgatory than to the hospital to see their mother. "Don't worry, I'll get a cab. I'll call you when I know my schedule and if there's a change in the meantime, call my cell phone." She repeated the number for him.

Would her mother want to see her? She had no idea. All she knew for certain was that she needed to see her mother.

* * *

Jean had forgotten over the space of years how truly miserable Dallas in September could be. The searing heat married to the high humidity was a palpable presence that pressed down on her as if she were under a steam iron. The cab from the airport to the hospital had been air-conditioned and the hospital corridors were cool beige tile, but just the short walk from the outside drop-off to the building had wilted her.

The nurses station was a desk in the shape of a hexagon. The patient rooms were arranged around the desk like spokes of a wheel. She asked to make sure she had the right number and stood for a moment outside the door, gathering her nerve to go inside.

Her stepfather was sitting in a chair next to the hospital bed. He looked up as she came in and said, "Jean. You're here."

She went to hug him and she felt him tremble. When she pulled away, he looked as if he'd aged twenty years. He had always had fair hair and pale skin but now he looked more like a ghost. The lines in his face had deepened and his pale eyes were watery, rimmed in red. She exclaimed, "Ron. Are you okay?"

"I'm okay. I'm so glad you're here." He tilted his head toward the bed. "I know Edie is glad you're here."

"Have you heard from Bobby?"

"He called. He'll be here soon."

Jean felt her lips compress into a tight line. She'd made it from Tesóro to Denver to the Dallas-Fort Worth airport faster than her brother could manage the drive from Houston. But she knew no comment from her would do any good. Bobby had always been their mother's favorite. She turned to the hospital bed.

Her mother was propped up on a couple of pillows, an IV line in one arm, heart and oxygen monitors hooked to the other. The carefully colored blond hair was in disarray, pushed up against the pillowcase. Without makeup her face looked as yellow as old newsprint.

Her eyes were open—the one eye Jean could see, anyway. The eyelid drooped over her right eye. She seemed alert but Jean couldn't tell how conscious she was.

Jean went to her and carefully touched a free spot on her arm. "Hello, Mother."

The eye she could see swiveled toward her. Ron said in an artificially cheery tone, "Look who's here, Edie. It's Jeanie, come to see you."

Jean drew in a deep breath, readying the speech she had rehearsed on the plane. "I'm sorry this happened to you," she said quietly. "I know we haven't been close and we don't agree on a lot of things, but you're my mother and I want you to get better soon."

In a voice that was still too loud, Ron said, "She's going to get better. The doctors said she can start speech therapy soon and physical therapy to help her walk again. You're going to be fine, aren't you, Edie?"

The eye shifted to Ron, then back to Jean. What was she thinking? Jean wondered. It almost didn't matter that her mother couldn't tell them what her thoughts were because Jean had never fathomed what she was thinking anyway. She'd never said to Jean, "I'm disappointed in you." She'd also never said, "I'm proud of you." At least not to her daughter. The club of disapproval had always been a silent one: a look of unhappiness when Jean had preferred jeans to skirts, or a grimace of distaste when Jean refused to go through the ritual of becoming a debutante. And when Jean had come out to her, her mother had said nothing at all, just turned away from her daughter without a word.

Now she had no words to give Jean had she wanted to speak them. Was this some kind of strange karma coming back to settle the score with her mother? Or was everything that happened just random, meaningless?

Jean had a sudden image of Lea and wondered what her answer would be. That she would have some kind of answer, Jean had no doubt.

Jean touched her mother's arm again. "He's right, Mother. You'll have to work hard and you'll get better. Keep on believing that."

Was her mother's crippled expression reflecting a note of gratitude? Or was it resignation, a belief that despite all the encouraging words, Edie Kraft knew her fate was already fixed?

Jean suppressed a shudder. How short life was and how much pain that short life could hold. She wondered if her mother had had any actual joy from her life, with her drinking and her parade of men.

Ron sat down again and they talked for a while about inconsequential things, Jean's new job, the hot weather, always including Edie in the conversation despite her inability to participate. After a few minutes, Jean kissed her mother on the forehead and said goodbye, promising a return visit in the evening.

She stepped outside the room. To her dismay, she saw her brother Bobby waiting for her at the nurses station. *I could have done without this*, she sighed.

He'd put on a good thirty pounds since she'd seen him last—how long ago? Almost ten years, she calculated. Worse, the comb-over he'd resorted to wasn't covering his sallow scalp. She realized with a jolt how much the shape of his face looked like their mother's. The broad forehead tapered quickly to low cheekbones and fell away to a chin that almost receded.

"Bobby," she greeted him coolly.

His mouth twisted. "What the he—what are you doing here?"

"Mom had a stroke. Had you heard?" She couldn't help herself.

He stepped closer, using his height and bulk as he always had to take up space and intimidate. Jean held herself in place with an effort. "You know what I mean," he said, his voice a snarl of disapproval. "Why bother to show up now? Sniffing around for her money?"

Jean wanted to laugh. "She doesn't have any money, Bobby. Ron has all the money there is. I came to see her."

"She doesn't need you," he barked. "You took off, left her. Go away. She doesn't need your kind."

"My kind of what?" Jean demanded. She knew she should walk away. Engaging Bobby never produced anything but anger and frustration.

His mouth twisted again. "You want me to announce it to the whole floor? My sister the dyke. The queer."

Jean tried to keep her anger reined in. "Make all the announcements you want, Bobby. You haven't changed, apparently, so tell anyone you like. You tell everybody I'm a dyke and I'll follow up with the announcement that you're a moronic bigot. Both statements will be equally true."

She expected him to start screaming but he surprised her. He drew back a fist like a club and swung at her.

Jean managed to partially turn away from the blow. It caught her on the shoulder. She could hear shouting behind Bobby at the nurses desk.

The swing made him stagger into her and Jean's instincts took over. She brought her knee up sharply. She felt it bounce off his thigh to pay dirt. It wasn't clean contact but it was enough for him to twist away, crouching in pain.

"Jesus!" he shouted. "You fucking bitch!"

Within a moment two men and a woman wearing scrubs had firm holds on his arms. Someone else was yelling into a phone demanding that security make an immediate appearance. Visitors and a couple of patients began to pour out of rooms in confusion.

A nurse approached her. "Are you hurt?" she demanded.

Jean shook her head, amazed at how hard she was breathing after a fight that had lasted less than ten seconds. "Fine. I'm fine."

Bobby was still cursing at her loudly. "Shut up, man, this is a hospital," one of the men muttered to him, but as Bobby's tirade continued, Jean dug into her pocket and produced her cell phone. She punched a few buttons and held the screen out in front of her.

Bobby was literally spitting with pain and rage. After another few seconds of profanity, Jean said calmly, "Thanks, Bobby. I'll be sure to post the video online just as soon as I get back to my laptop."

He snapped his jaws shut as Jean smiled at him.

The Pennington restaurant was blessedly cool, filled with green plants and crisp white linens. Jean was on her second glass of iced tea when she saw a small woman approaching from the hostess station.

Her friend had changed very little in the years since they'd left school. She was dressed in a silk blend suit tailored to fit her petite frame and she was carrying a handbag that cost more than Jean's entire ensemble, never mind the small fortune she must have paid for her shoes. Jean rose from the table and gave her a hug that nearly squeezed her breathless.

"Hey, Jean," Maryke exclaimed. "I might break if you keep that up."

"Sorry." Jean was shamefaced. "It's just been so long. I'm so glad you could come today."

"It has been too long," she agreed. Neither of them mentioned that their last face-to-face meeting was Charlotte's funeral. "I was so sorry to hear about Edie."

They sat down and Jean drank in the sight of her oldest friend. "You look great, Maryke."

Jean pronounced it as "Mar-ée-ka" and the other woman sighed happily. "It's such a pleasure to hear my name pronounced correctly again. All day I have to explain to clients that it's not 'Mary Kay' or 'Marky.'"

"You need to blame your mom for that."

Maryke smoothed back her dark hair, which was still in a perfect French knot. "Actually, I blame Dad. He's the one who let Mom dig up a genuine Dutch family name and stick it on me." She rolled her eyes but smiled. "Actually, it's a lot of fun at programmer conventions on my nametag. Every guy I meet is trying to figure out how to pronounce it by staring at my chest."

"You just like men staring at you."

"True. Very true." Maryke sighed with pleasure. "I'm sorry for the reason, but I'm really happy to see you in person. Email and phone calls just aren't the same."

Jean reached across the table and grasped her hand briefly. "I'm really glad to see you too."

When the waiter appeared, Maryke ordered without having to open the menu. She ate here at least once a week and had all of her choices memorized, Jean knew. Jean settled for a Cobb salad.

"So how is your Mother?" Maryke asked.

Jean grew somber. "It's going to be a long road back for her. She has what the doctors call expressive aphasia, which essentially means she can't talk other than gibberish. They don't know yet if she has other brain damage."

"I imagine that would be difficult to tell until they can figure out how to communicate with her," Maryke said dryly.

Jean almost smiled. Her friend was still the least sentimental person she'd ever met. Jean hadn't been surprised when Maryke took to computer programming like a bird to the air. Yet through all the turbulent years of Jean's youth, Maryke had always been Jean's supporter, an impartial listener and dispenser of sound advice. She'd supported Jean's decision to leave Charlotte at the end and had been the first one on the plane to California when Charlotte died.

"I've really missed you," Jean said simply.

"Of course you have," Maryke replied. "Who wouldn't? I'm lovely, charming, intelligent and incredibly insightful."

Jean laughed. "After the morning I've had, I didn't think it was possible that anyone could make me laugh. Even you."

"Told you I was charming." Maryke eyed her critically. "Did something happen other than seeing your mother?"

Jean sighed. She was saved from immediate response when their meals arrived. Maryke was having the Pennington's signature shrimp salad, the plump pink shellfish layered with avocado. "That looks great," Jean said. "I miss how plentiful—and relatively cheap—avocados were in California."

"What's the local specialty in Desert Wasteland, Colorado?" Maryke asked.

Chewing her lip, Jean responded, "Green chile cheeseburgers."

"Sounds delightfully ethnic."

"Snob. They're delicious."

"If you say so. And you didn't answer my question. What else happened today?"

"Bobby happened," Jean muttered.

Maryke sat back in her chair. "You should have let me run him down in your driveway when we were eighteen."

Jean laughed again. "It would have ruined your brand-new graduation present from your parents."

"The rear end damage to the BMW would have been worth it." She batted her mascara-laden eyelashes. "'Oh my, officer, the sun was in my eyes and I didn't see the creepy bastard trying to cross the driveway.'"

"It was noon, Maryke. I doubt if the 'sun was in my eyes' excuse would have worked."

Maryke waved a dismissive hand. "Oh, please. Have you no faith in my persuasive abilities?"

"I have infinite faith in your persuasive abilities."

"So what happened with Bobby, the creepy bastard?"

"He tried to punch me outside Mother's hospital room."

Maryke's fork hit her salad plate with a clatter. "What? Are you okay?"

"I'm fine." She briefly described the encounter, which had ended with hospital security escorting Bobby off the property.

"You should have had his fat ass arrested," Maryke remarked, picking up her fork again.

Jean cleared her throat. "I did something just about as good," she said. She showed Maryke the brief video, turning down the sound so that the Pennington's staff wouldn't feel compelled to throw them out before they'd finished their salads.

Maryke smirked. "Well, that's just delightful. What's your plan?"

"I thought I'd post it online."

Her friend tapped the tines of her fork against the rim of her plate. "Send it to me," Maryke said at length. "I have a couple of thoughts."

"You don't have to deal with him."

"Are you serious? It would be my pleasure." She looked thoughtful for a moment. "Who's that idiot minister at that cult he goes to?"

"Pastor Johns. He's the guy who has deemed my lesbian soul unfit for heaven."

Maryke nodded. "Leave it to me. You know, I wish I'd had anything remotely so juicy on either of my ex-husbands."

Jean's Cobb salad was delicious, the ratio of meat and cheese perfectly balanced with the lettuce. The dressing was housemade buttermilk ranch, fresh and tangy. She told herself once again that it was time to start eating better and cooking at home.

"So, which of the prospects you mentioned in your last email are you actually dating?" she asked Maryke.

"Dating, hmm. The word is so passé at my age. Rather, you should ask if I'm getting any."

Jean tried not to choke on the piece of hard-boiled egg halfway down her throat. "Okay then. Are you getting any?"

Maryke sighed. "Not nearly enough. I'm seeing the guy who works as a programmer for NovaComp. He's twenty-eight so I thought he'd be a little more focused about getting some action between the sheets, but he's some kind of workaholic."

"Just like somebody else I could name," Jean interjected.

"Very funny. Half the time he seems more interested in his computer monitor than my tits."

This time Jean avoided the choking hazard by continuing to chew. "Not to say 'what's sauce for the goose is sauce for the gander,' but—"

"Oh, shut up," Maryke said good-naturedly. "If he doesn't start generating a little more gusto in the bedroom, I'm going to have to trade him in on a younger model. I'll find some guy still in the throes of hormonal enthusiasm."

"Great. Just make sure he's over age eighteen."

"You're always such a lawyer. How about I find a twenty-one-year-old? Then I can say with complete truth that I'm dating a man half my age."

"Something I know you always aspired to do."

"So true." Maryke placed fork and knife across her nearly empty plate and a waiter immediately appeared to whisk it away. "So what about you, Jean?"

Jean drank iced tea. "What about me?"

"Oh, stop being coy. You haven't mentioned anyone. Are you dating yet?"

She hesitated over the answer and saw Maryke's eyes narrow. "Does that moment of silence mean yes?" Maryke demanded.

"No."

"Does that 'no' mean you're *not* dating?"

"Not really."

"Stop stalling and tell me all."

Jean began slowly, "There's a woman—"

"Yes," Maryke said dryly, "I figured that part out. I've known you liked girls since the seventh grade."

"What?" Jean interrupted her own story. "I didn't come out to you until we were juniors in high school."

"Honey, by that time you were just telling me what I knew already, believe me. And believe this too, I was very happy about it. It meant there was less competition for the limited number of guys who were both smart enough to date and didn't wear pocket protectors. I always figured we'd have the same type. Imagine my relief and delight when you seemed to prefer various members of the girls' field hockey team. Now, come on. Out with it. Who is this woman you're not really dating?"

Jean cleared her throat and tried to decide what to say. "I met her at work."

"Oh, jeez, not another lawyer, I hope."

"No. She's the sheriff."

Maryke rubbed her hands together. "Well, that sounds promising. A woman in uniform. Let me guess, she's the strong and silent sort?"

"Why would you say that?" Jean's curiosity sparked.

Maryke snorted. "Honey, apparently it's my task today to enlighten you. Here's more news for you. You do definitely have a type."

"Charlotte wasn't like that," Jean defended herself.

Giving her an assessing look for a moment, Maryke said, "Are we far enough away from Charlotte that I can tell you what I really want to say?"

Jean looked at her in surprise. "Maryke, when did you ever hesitate to say what you really wanted to say?"

"Well, there was no point in my telling you anything about Charlotte. You were determined to save her from herself and nothing I could have said to you would have convinced you otherwise."

Jean's surprise deepened. Was that really true? Had she been so swept up in her life with Charlotte that she'd been unable to see what she really had been doing?

"She was never what you needed, Jean," Maryke continued. "You need someone as strong as you are yourself and Charlotte was never even close."

"I'm not strong," Jean demurred.

"Bullshit," Maryke rejoined quickly. "You actually survived a chaotic childhood with your brains and heart intact. I always thought—" She stopped abruptly, hesitating.

"Go on," Jean said bravely.

Maryke sighed. "I always thought that was the attraction for you. With Charlotte, I mean. She was an emotional mess and that was what you were used to, after all."

Jean stared at her friend for a minute or two. Finally she said, "Are you saying I fell for someone just like my mother?"

Maryke laughed and Jean could sense relief in her tone. "In a way. Don't worry, we all do it. Derek was about as close to my father as I could have found in a man forty years younger."

"That explains husband number one. What was your excuse for Remy?" Jean asked.

"What do you think? You saw him, the man was gorgeous and the sex was amazing. You cannot imagine what that man could do in bed."

"You're right," Jean acknowledged. "I can't imagine and if I could, I wouldn't be interested in it."

Maryke tilted her head to one side. "You know, it's funny. I can certainly imagine having sex with another woman. I can even imagine enjoying it, as a sort of change of pace. But lesbians can't see themselves with a guy?"

"I speak only for myself when I say definitively, ick," Jean answered promptly. "One attempted kiss from Stevie Carter in seventh grade was plenty of heterosexual experience for me."

"This trip down the memory lane of our love lives is all very interesting, but could we get back to the sheriff, please?" Maryke said. "Perhaps you could explain how you're dating but not dating her?"

Jean glanced away and sighed again. "We've been out a few times, but it was never really an official date. A couple of lunches, mostly about work. A dinner once with some other people. A horseback ride. And a dance."

Maryke's eyebrows drew together in a gentle frown. "Really. You've been dancing with her but you're *not* dating her? What in the hell is the matter with you? Is she a moron or something? Or doesn't she do anything for your libido?"

Jean cleared her throat. "She's as smart as I am. Which makes her much smarter than you."

"You are just hysterically funny today. And you failed to answer the question about your libido. Aren't you attracted to her?"

Jean fiddled with her unused knife on the tablecloth. "Okay, yes. Very much attracted."

"Then what the hell is the problem? Oh shit, she's not single. God, you lesbians pair up like you were getting on Noah's ark. Not that you would have been invited onto Noah's ark, of course."

"No, she's single, several years out of a relationship," Jean admitted.

"Okay, I give up. Single, smart and she rings your bell. What on earth is the problem?"

"It's me, Maryke," Jean confessed. "I'm afraid I just don't have anything left to give to anybody. I told her I don't have what it takes anymore to be in a relationship. Charlotte took it all." After a moment she added, "The nightmares are back sometimes. It's guilt, I think, because I couldn't save her."

They were quiet for a minute, the soft sounds of conversation and the muted clattering of plates and silverware flowing around them. At length Maryke said, "You're giving up on this because of Charlotte?"

Jean nodded.

"That's the biggest load of bullshit I've ever heard from you, Jean, and believe me that's going some."

Jean looked up at her in shock. "What do you mean?"

"I mean just what I said. That's plain and simple crap. You get to grieve for Charlotte but what are you going to do, live the rest of your life like a nun?"

"That's what Lea said," Jean admitted. "Although she was a lot more tactful about it than you were."

"Well, no shit. A bulldozer is more tactful than I am. Now stop being such a coward. Go home and tell this Lea person you were wrong and give it try. For Pete's sake, what have you got to lose?"

"It's not that simple," Jean said softly.

"You know what?" Maryke responded sharply. "You're wrong. It is just that simple. Here's a news bulletin for you. You can't change the past, kiddo, and you can't control the future. All you can do is make today the best you can. Don't be an idiot, Jean."

"And *carpe diem* to you too," Jean muttered.

"Hey, it's a cliché because it's true. I'm not telling you to run off to Canada and marry the woman. But give her a chance. Give yourself a chance."

"What is it with you?" Jean asked in bewilderment. "Why the hard sell all of a sudden?"

"Because I haven't heard you talk about anyone in all this time since Charlotte died. And because I love you, you moron, and I want you to be happy."

"Maryke, I don't think I can have my heart broken again."

"I hope to God she won't do that, but you know what? You'll survive. I've had mine broken more than once and I'm still here, still in there fighting. You can do anything you want except give up on love. End of speech."

Jean sat back in her chair, shaking her head. "What am I going to do with you?"

"Keep me on your Christmas card list, so when you start sending out family photos of you and the sheriff and your lovely household of dogs or cats or parakeets or whatever the hell you lesbians collect, I can laugh smugly and say I told you so. Oh and you can pay for lunch too."

CHAPTER TEN

On the plane ride back from Dallas Saturday morning, Jean spent the flight staring out the window at Kansas thousands of feet below, thinking about Maryke's advice. Not really advice as much as marching orders, Jean thought ruefully.

When she left Colorado to return to Texas, Jean had been uncertain whether she could be with Lea. She was afraid. It might not be fair to Lea, she told herself. Lea deserved someone better, someone whole, someone whose heart hadn't been shattered. It would be like asking Lea to pay full price for a broken vase that had been glued back together.

But Maryke's words had gotten her attention and Jean was even more shaken by the sight of her stricken mother. Life could be short and you never knew when it might end. She wondered again if Charlotte had really intended for that night to be her last on earth.

Maybe she should take a chance. God knew Lea was everything she thought she might want in a woman. Wasn't it worth a try? Even if it ended badly, how could she be much more miserable than she'd been in the dark days after Charlotte's death? And perhaps this time she could find someone to love the way she longed to love.

Lunch, she decided. She'd call Lea as soon as she got back and invite her to lunch. She would tell Lea she had been wrong, she was willing to go out, to see if they might be compatible. Trepidation the size of monarch butterflies fluttered up from her belly as she thought about seeing Lea again. This had to be the right decision. They could go slowly, take their time. She didn't have to commit to anything before she was ready. It would be better this time. It would be good between them. The promise of the kiss on the little mesa had to mean something, didn't it?

She retrieved her car from the long-term parking lot at Denver International and began the hour-and-a-half drive south on the Valley Highway. As she neared the downtown exit for her condo, she checked the time and considered. If she stopped by the office now to check her messages and mail, it would save her time on Monday morning and make her feel better about taking Sunday completely off. Maybe she didn't have to wait until Monday to call Lea. If she called her this evening, perhaps they could see each other tomorrow.

The thought cheered her up and she decided an hour or so at the office was worth it.

The elected officials, department heads and a few select other employees had reserved parking spaces in the basement of the main county building. Del had managed to get reserved spots for all the attorneys in his office, though the paralegals and support staff had to park in the county-leased parking lot half a block down the street. Jean found her access card in her purse and got in through the parking garage gate. Her parking spot was next to Del's space.

As she pulled in she noticed a car two spaces away. All the parking spaces in this section were for the county attorney's office. Jean wondered who was working on Saturday afternoon. One of the advantages of being a lawyer in the public sector instead of private practice, she had found, was that the hours were more humane. Big law firms expected weekend work but government offices nearly always worked regular eight to four thirty, five days a week.

As she passed by the parked car—a small Toyota, she noted—she saw that the passenger-side window was rolled down.

Jean frowned. It wasn't hot enough to justify leaving a window down. The lighting was poor in the garage, so she leaned into the open window to see if the driver had left his or her keys in the ignition.

Todd Moorman was sitting in the driver's seat, leaning forward on the steering wheel as if he were sleeping.

"Todd?"

She reached across to touch his shoulder. He shifted slightly. Then Jean saw that his eyes were closed, but not in sleep. Because of the large, dark hole in his temple. Dried blood caked his cheek and jaw and beyond him on the closed driver's-side window, Jean could see streaks of more blood. Bits of white bone and pale pink-gray smears that had to be bits of brain.

Nausea seized her. The picture of Todd's body blurred before her eyes until all she could see was Charlotte lying pale across their ivory duvet with scarlet rivulets of blood marring her arms and the silk beneath her.

Jean jerked out of the car. She managed a few steps before bending over to empty whatever breakfast was left in her stomach.

* * *

The nondescript detective whose name she couldn't quite remember—Morton? Miller?—asked her, "Do you have your ticket with you?"

For a confused moment Jean thought he meant a parking receipt, then realized he was referring to her airplane ticket. She dug the e-ticket receipt out of her purse.

She was sitting in the back of a Tesóro police car while the crime scene processing swirled on around them. A technician, justifiably unhappy with the lighting, had set up a couple of bright white lights that made the underground parking lot look bright as the middle of an afternoon on the Fourth of July. They'd finally started to remove Todd's body from his car and Jean quickly looked away.

She had already given them permission to search her car and her purse. They'd found her suitcase in the trunk and now the detective was carefully examining her e-ticket receipt.

"May I keep this for a while?" he asked. "I need to confirm you were on the flight."

"Of course," Jean said automatically. Somewhere among telling her story four times she'd finally figured out that her flight gave her an alibi. Todd had certainly been dead more than just a couple of hours and if she was in Dallas, she couldn't have killed him. The police were obviously trying to eliminate her, the person who found him, as a suspect.

"Detective…"

"It's Munson."

"Yes, Detective Munson. What happened? I mean, I know you can't be certain, but although I've only known Todd a few months, he was the most innocuous man I've ever met. The last person I thought would have been a murder victim. I don't suppose it could have been suicide?"

He shook his head. "We haven't recovered the gun. It's hard to get rid of one after you shoot yourself in the head."

"I just can't imagine why anyone would want to kill him."

He shrugged. "Maybe it wasn't personal."

"A robbery?"

"Yeah. Or I'm thinking attempted carjacking."

"On a weekend afternoon?" Jean asked skeptically.

"He probably died last night sometime. Gotta wait for the coroner's report."

That made more sense to Jean than a deliberate murder aimed at Todd, but she was so emotionally drained from the week she didn't ask any other questions.

The afternoon faded into evening before she got home after questions, searches and signing her statement. Despite her exhaustion, sleep was a long time coming. The replay of finding

Todd's body seemed merged inextricably with Charlotte's death. Faint gray streaks of impending dawn were rimming her window blinds before she finally fell into troubled sleep.

The moment she stepped into the reception area of the county attorney's office Monday morning she realized that someone had spread the news of Todd's death. Everyone was clustered around Rita's desk. A couple of the women were crying and the men looked shell-shocked. Jean moved toward them swiftly.

Rita stood up so that she could see Jean. Her eyes were rimmed in red and she used a tissue to wipe her cheeks. "We just heard about Todd," she answered. "Do you—"

"I know," Jean interrupted. "I'm sorry I wasn't here early enough to tell all of you myself."

Rita said, "I heard it on the radio driving in this morning. I couldn't believe it."

One of the women began crying louder, saying, "But he was so young!" Someone led her away. The others hovered around Rita's desk, reluctant to stay but unable to make themselves leave.

"Does anybody know what happened?" one of the men asked. "All Rita told us was that they found him in his car in the office parking lot."

Jean sighed, trying to delay the inevitable disclosure. "That's right."

Rita cocked her head a little. "Did you talk to the sheriff about it? Can you tell us any more about what happened?"

Jean perched on the edge of Rita's desk and addressed the worried faces around her. "I didn't find out anything from the sheriff, but you'll hear soon enough. I was the one who found him."

The announcement was met with more frowns and soft gasps. Rita exclaimed, "Oh, no! How awful for you, Jean."

The mental picture came back to her, turning her stomach sour. She wished more than anything that she could wipe from her memory the vision of the abstract painting splatter that was Todd's blood, bone and brains on the driver's-side window.

She told them what little she knew, omitting the worst of the details. "The police seemed to think it was a carjacking gone bad. They think Todd resisted and the car thief shot him."

As she said it, Jean realized that the scenario seemed unlikely. Wouldn't a carjacker approach the driver's-side window? And why would Todd roll down the passenger-side window to a stranger?

One of the paralegals said in a trembling voice, "Do you think we're safe? Going to the parking lot?"

"The police assured me they'll be doing extra patrols to check the area. Until they catch the person who did this, they recommend that no one walk to the parking lot alone."

"The buddy system," one of the men said.

"Yes. Check with each other before leaving for the day for a while, okay?"

There were nods all around. Jean glanced around and asked, "Where's the boss?"

"He went upstairs to tell the board," Rita answered sadly. "He said he'd find out about the arrangements and let us know."

Typical of him to leave his staff alone at a crisis moment like this, Jean thought. "This is terrible news for all of us," she said to the group. "Maggie, put the phones back on the off-hours recording for a few minutes and let's all go into the break room, okay?"

She led them into the small room that housed the coffeemaker, microwave, printers and the copier. Everyone who could find a seat sat down and the others crowded around.

"I feel awful about Todd," she said simply. "And I know all of you do too. He was a genuinely nice guy and this is a horrible and senseless tragedy. I know we'll all grieve for him in our own ways. What I'd like to suggest is that we do our best to try to go back to work for a while. When Del gets back, I'll talk to him about closing the office—if not today, then perhaps on the day of Todd's funeral or memorial service. Maybe we could all go together, as an office."

This plan seemed to meet with general approval, several nodding heads giving their support. Jean continued, "We'll take up a collection and make an office gesture of some kind, flowers or a contribution to his church or favorite charity."

"I'll start the envelope around," Rita added quietly.

Jean gave her a grateful smile. "Thanks. I know it will be hard not to think about Todd today, so we'll just do the best we can. If anyone needs to talk to me, I'll be in the office all day."

"Can you find out what's going on with the investigation?" someone asked. "Have they arrested anybody or even have any suspects?"

"I don't know the answers, but I'll see what I can do," Jean promised. "If I find anything out, I'll send out an email. Okay, guys, thanks."

After everyone else filed out, Rita stayed behind. She said softly, "I'm so sorry you had to come back to this, Jean. How's your mother?"

"She's out of immediate danger. It's nice of you to ask. There will be a lot of rehab for her." Jean shook her head. "Rita, this is unbelievable. Todd Moorman had to be the least offensive man on the planet. Who would kill him? And for his car, for God's sake?"

"People kill for less than that," Rita answered sadly.

"I know. I know they do, but it's still just, well, unbelievable."

Jean sat in her office a long time, staring at the pile of mail neatly stacked on her desk, seeing the blinking red light on her office phone. The work called to her but she had trouble getting going. How was she supposed to care about phone messages and emails when Todd was dead?

She shook herself and began to tackle the work. She cleared out her emails first, deleting most, forwarding a few and saving the three that needed a personal response. It constantly amazed her how few of the emails she received were actually important or relevant.

The stack of snail mail came next. Most envelopes contained copies of court documents that went into the "To Be Filed" tray on the corner of her credenza. A couple of letters that needed response went into the "In" basket. The most recent America Bar Association journal was set aside in the pile of professional material that she rarely seemed to have time to actually read. Everything else went directly into the recycling bin tucked in the corner.

Jean saved the voice mail for last. The telephone was her least favorite way of communicating at work. The written word was less susceptible to being misinterpreted or forgotten than conversations and she nearly always wished people would send her an email instead of calling her. Nevertheless, it was true that lots of clients still preferred to leave her voice-mail messages. With a sigh, she opened the notebook where she kept a phone log and hit the replay button.

Nine calls. Not too bad for four working days out of the office. As she went through them, jotting down names and numbers while noting the times of the calls, she prioritized them.

The three calls from outside attorneys would have to be returned later today. The one Del had forwarded to her would come first. County Clerk Netta Telford had called as well. Her problem would require a few minutes of research that Jean could delegate to their intern, but Jean would have to return the call to Netta personally. Del's rule was that elected officials always got a phone call from her or from Del personally, one of the rules he had that made sense to her.

Human Resources had a quick question about a time sheet Jean had signed before she left and Purchasing had another problem with a contract that needed resolution. She returned both calls immediately and got them off her to-do list within a few minutes. She then forwarded a call from a vendor to Rita, hoping her paralegal would be able to answer some critically important question about their copier paper.

That left two calls from Friday. The first came in just before six that evening.

"Jean, it's Lea. I just had a chance to talk to Rita. She told me your mother was ill and you had to leave town. I'm sorry I didn't know sooner. If you need anything, please let me know." There was a brief moment of hesitation on the recording before Lea continued, "Call me when you get back and let me know how you're doing."

That was all, but Jean played the message twice over just to listen to the warmth in Lea's voice and the concern in her tone. Some part of Jean had been afraid that after their last conversation, Lea would be angry with her or upset. She found herself relieved that Lea still seemed concerned about her. Not that she was surprised, really. Lea didn't seem like a woman to be petty or to have feelings that were easy to hurt. Jean admired her for that.

Jean finally erased the message without writing it down. She would remember to call Lea later without a reminder. She punched the button to listen to the last voice mail. It had come in at six thirty-five Friday evening.

"Um, Jean, hi, it's Todd. Look, I now you're gone and everything, but I thought you might check in and, ah, if you do, will you call me? I'm leaving the office now but anytime you get this message call me. We need to talk about the job, I think."

He rattled off his cell phone number and hung up. Jean sat staring at the phone a moment and then played the dead man's voice again.

Six thirty-five. Todd had been shot in the parking lot Friday evening, probably minutes after leaving this message. She tried not to shudder at the thought.

What did the message mean? She couldn't think what was so important that he wanted her to call him over the weekend. What job was he talking about?

Maybe his own job, she thought. Perhaps he knew he was in trouble at work and that she wasn't happy with his performance, although she couldn't imagine how he would have figured that out for himself. She hadn't mentioned it to anyone and Jean doubted he had enough insight to see her displeasure. Perhaps he'd had a job offer from somewhere else? That seemed highly unlikely to her and even if it were true, wouldn't he talk to Del instead?

She puzzled over it a few minutes more, but nothing came to her. The dilemma of what to do with the message remained. The content of the voice mail probably didn't mean anything, but it occurred to her that it might at least establish some part of Todd's schedule that evening for the police. She saved the message just in case and then picked up the phone.

She'd known to call the Tesóro Police Department on Saturday because the San Carlos County Sheriff's Office only had enforcement jurisdiction in the unincorporated parts of the county. She could just call the detective at Tesóro directly, but her self-restraint in not talking to Lea for forty-eight hours was gone by now. She dialed Lea's office number.

Lea's assistant Vicki answered the office phone and said, not surprisingly, that Lea was out of the office. Jean left a message and then debated whether to call Lea's cell phone. She finally decided Todd's voice mail was important enough to justify the call and she dug out her own cell. Her office phone number wouldn't show up on Lea's caller ID and she wanted Lea to know who was calling.

"Hawkins," Lea answered crisply. "Are you all right, Jean?"

"I'm fine," she said. "I know you're out of the office. Is it a bad time?"

"I would say yes to that," Lea said. "And I'll need to call you back later. But I got a call from Tesóro PD this morning. Courtesy call about a murdered county employee. Did you hear about it?"

"Oh, God, Lea. I know we have a lot to talk about, but I need to tell you something important."

She could hear Lea restraining her impatience. "All right," she conceded.

She thinks it's personal, Jean thought. She hesitated for a long moment and then heard Lea's phone end the call. Jean quickly dialed back and when Lea answered again, Jean asked, "Did you hang up? You didn't say anything."

"Sorry," Lea said. "I always feel like an idiot yelling 'are you still there?' into a phone. I thought the call had been dropped."

Jean said quickly, "I have to tell you that I'm the one who found Todd's body. I decided to come into the office after I flew back on Saturday and saw his car in the lot and…"

She stopped, unable to continue. Lea said, "Jean, I am so sorry. Do I need to rearrange my schedule? I can be back at your office within the hour."

Lea was offering to leave work to be with her? Jean's earlier distress faded with the sound of the worry in Lea's voice. "I'm all right," Jean said. "And I know you're busy. I called because even though I know your office isn't handling Todd Moorman's murder investigation, I have some information that might be of some help."

"What is it?"

As she explained about Todd's voice-mail message, she heard people talking loudly at Lea's end of the phone call and then the noise faded as Lea presumably moved away.

Lea said, "You should absolutely talk to the detective assigned to the case. It will help to establish the time line of the evening. I'll have…"

"Detective Munson," she supplied.

"I'll have him call you back about this within the hour," Lea said shortly. "If you're sure you're okay—"

"I'm fine."

"Then we'll have to talk later."

She hung up and Jean put the phone down on her desktop, wondering how she could ever have thought it was a good idea to turn down the chance to date Lea.

Jean returned to her list of work for the day. She made an effort not to think about Todd or her mother and especially not about Sheriff Lea Hawkins.

It was midafternoon before the detective from Tesóro PD showed up in her office with a worried-looking Rita at his elbow. "There's a police officer here to see you," Rita announced unnecessarily.

"Hello, Detective Munson," she greeted him.

She hadn't really seen him clearly last night, in the shock of her discovery. She'd never met a man who looked more like a basset hound. Faded brown hair cut short didn't conceal his long ears with the largest earlobes she'd ever seen. They complemented his heavy jowls and wrinkled neck. Jean just managed not to look for the dog collar above his tie. His manner was as lugubrious as his face appeared. Jean wondered if he looked doleful because that was his personality or whether it was the other way around.

"I hope it was all right that I called the sheriff's office first," Jean said. "I wasn't sure if I needed to bother you with this."

"Did you remember something else from that night?" Munson asked.

"No. I had a telephone call from Todd, probably the night he was killed." Jean played the message for him and he took careful notes. Then he produced a small digital tape recorder and had her play the message again while he made his own recording.

"How long can you save this voice mail on your system?" he asked.

"Messages are usually expunged after ninety days, but I can ask our IT department to save it longer for you." Jean was pleased that she'd made the call to Information Technology to discover this information before the detective arrived.

He nodded, his jowls bouncing up and down in slow motion. "Ask them to save it. We made need it later. You're sure it's his voice, I assume."

"Without a doubt."

He pulled at one elongated earlobe. "So what was this job he was talking about?"

"I have no idea," Jean admitted.

He gave her a mournful look, as if he'd already known she wouldn't be able to help him. They spent a few minutes going over everything else she knew about Todd, which didn't amount to very much. She didn't think the information that Todd knotted his neckties badly would be very helpful in solving his murder.

"May I ask you a question?" Jean said as he stuffed his notebook and recorder back into his shapeless brown suit jacket.

"You can ask," he said reluctantly.

"Was it really a carjacking?" The more she thought about the scene, the less likely it seemed to her. Of course, the thought that someone had killed Todd deliberately seemed equally improbable to her.

Munson shrugged. "No way of knowing. His wallet was still there and his wedding ring was still on his finger, so it's hard to tell whether it was really a robbery or not."

Jean winced. She'd forgotten that Todd was married. "His poor wife," she murmured aloud.

The detective gave her a gloomy expression. "Yeah, she took it pretty hard."

"Do you have any suspects?" Jean asked.

"I can't really discuss that with you," he answered as he lumbered to his feet. He offered a doleful handshake and said, "Thanks for your help."

After he had gone, Jean got up and restlessly paced her office, idly straightening the books on her shelves as she thought about Todd Moorman. Something was niggling at the back of her mind, something important that had been driven into hibernation by her unexpected trip to Dallas and her focus on her relationship with Lea.

Worrying about it wasn't going to make it easier to remember, she decided. Better to let it percolate in her brain for a while to see if the thought could come to the surface. She sat down at her desk again and reached for a case file.

Case file. She'd given Todd the Lambert case file to review and asked his opinion about the viability of the lawsuit. Was that the job he'd been talking about? But what would have been so important that he'd asked her to call him over the weekend?

The last time she'd seen the file it had been stacked in the corner of Todd's office. Was it still there? If someone killed him for it, it seemed unlikely—but there was only one way she would know for certain.

She walked down the hall. After the police had done a routine search of Todd's office, someone had closed the door. As she expected, it was unlocked. None of the attorneys locked their offices, except for Del. She opened the door and went inside.

The Lambert case file was gone.

Jean stood frozen in the doorway, thoughts tumbling around in her mind like acrobats. It couldn't be a coincidence, could it? Maybe the file had nothing to do with Todd's death. Or maybe it had everything to do with it.

Jean searched Todd's office, desk, his file drawers, his bookcase stacked with statute books and files as well. The Lambert file was nowhere in the office.

She went back out and asked Rita if she knew anything about the Lambert file. "No, why?" Rita asked.

"I'll locate it," Jean reassured her as she headed back to her office.

Why was the file folder missing? There must have been something in it that triggered Todd's phone call to her, but what was it? If Todd wanted to talk to her about whatever he'd found in the folder, might he have taken the file home with him? The attorneys weren't supposed to remove the folders from the office, but maybe he'd thought it was important to break the rules.

Jean dug out the business card Detective Munson had given her and called the number. He was out but she left a detailed message on his voice mail, asking about any file folders in Todd's car or his briefcase.

There wasn't much else she could do today. It was time to go home.

* * *

It was close to nine o'clock that evening when her cell phone rang. Jean thought it might be Munson, but the caller ID told her it was Lea.

"Are you at home?" Lea's voice sounded weary.

"Yes," Jean said. "Sounds like you had a long day."

"You could say that. Look, I'm downtown at the office anyway. Could I stop by for a few minutes? Tomorrow doesn't look much better than today did but I'd like to see you."

Jean took a quick look around the condo. Her dinner dishes were still on the counter and there were several days' worth of newspapers on her coffee table. She sighed, knowing she'd want to see Lea even if the house was on fire. "Sure," she answered. "See you in a minute."

Jean managed to tuck the dishes into the dishwasher and dump the papers into the recycling bin before Lea's knock sounded. She couldn't do anything about her sweatpants and ancient T-shirt, but she did pull her hair back into a neat ponytail before she opened the door.

Lea looked as tired as she'd sounded on the phone. There were dark smudges under her eyes and her uniform was less than crisp, but when she saw Jean, she gave her a crooked smile. "Hi."

"Hi. Come on in."

Lea sat on the couch and sighed. "It feels like three days just since I got off my feet."

"Do you want some tea? Or coffee maybe?"

Lea hesitated. "Only if it's already made. I don't want you to go to any trouble."

"It'll take two minutes. You look like you could use something."

"Coffee, then," Lea said gratefully. "It's kind of a long drive home, as you know."

Jean brought out two mugs when the coffee had brewed. Lea had her head back with her eyes closed. Jean wondered if she'd fallen asleep but Lea sat up straight as Jean approached and took the coffee gratefully.

"Thanks," Lea said. "So tell me about your mother."

Jean went through the story and Lea listened without interruption, although she stirred at Jean's description of the altercation with her brother. "Didn't know geeky lawyers could mix it up, did you?" Jean asked, smiling.

"I'm not surprised in the least," Lea said. "He sounds like a jerk. I'm sorry I wasn't there."

"Me too. But it wasn't as bad as coming back and finding Todd…" Her voice trailed off.

Lea said, "We don't have to talk about it unless you want to."

"I really don't. So do you want to tell me about your day instead?"

Lea sighed. "Nope. Don't take it personally. It was just a bunch of stuff." Her expression softened and she said, "I really am sorry about your friend Todd."

"He wasn't really a friend, not really," Jean acknowledged. "But he was a colleague and a nice guy, though I didn't think he was particularly good at his job. But I need to tell you something else."

That got her an alert look. "About the murder?"

"I think so. The file I gave him to work on, the Lambert case? You remember the case where the man who was shot in his house had been suing the county? Well, the file folders have gone missing."

Lea drank her coffee, then said, "Let me get this straight. First Lambert is killed at his home, supposedly by our Joya burglar, but apparently not. Then the attorney who is working on the Lambert case is shot to death during what looks like a carjacking or a mugging? This is not a story that is making a lot of sense, but the deaths have to be connected. Two coincidental shootings is no coincidence."

"After I talked to Detective Munson about the phone call, I left a message with him to see if the file folders might have been in Todd's car."

"Good thinking. I'll call him tomorrow as well. Maybe Moorman's wife knows something. I'll ask him to check their house, just in case he took the files home sometime before Friday."

"You're convinced the two killings are connected?"

Lea gave her an appraising look. "Yes. Aren't you?"

Jean smiled ruefully. "You're the police officer here."

"You have a working brain," Lea responded. "Do you think they're *not* connected?"

Jean got up and began to pace around her living room. "I do, but I'll be damned if I can figure out how. Killing Lambert wouldn't stop the lawsuit from going forward, though it would certainly make the case more difficult to win, since Lambert himself wouldn't be available as a witness. But if someone were going to kill him for a reason connected with the lawsuit, they should have done so before he was deposed. And Todd wasn't going to try the case. He was just doing some research for me."

"Wait," Lea interjected. "Why would it matter whether Lambert was killed before or after his deposition?"

"Because a deposition is sworn testimony. His attorneys can admit it in court as evidence since his death makes him no longer available as a witness. It's a way to get his story in front of the jury. If somebody wanted to screw up the lawsuit, they should have shot him before he was deposed."

"Still, there must be something," Lea persisted. "The fact that the file is missing seems to be some indication that there was something in it that connects the Lambert case with Todd Moorman's murder."

"Okay," Jean conceded. "But I've been thinking about this all evening and I can't figure out what could possibly be in the file that could be a motive for a murder, let alone two murders."

Lea sighed. "I hope we'll be able to figure that out when—and if—we locate the file." She yawned and stretched. "Thanks for the coffee. I'm sorry I'm so exhausted. Are you sure you're all right? You've had a really rough week, between your mother and then coming back to all this."

Jean had a sudden urge to join her on the couch, wrap herself around Lea and hold on. Why had she been so resistant to becoming involved with her? Her reasons and her pain seemed to recede every moment she spent in Lea's presence.

But Lea was already headed for the door and now wasn't the time to explain her change of heart. Instead she said, "Let's talk tomorrow. Dinner, maybe? If you have time."

Lea gave her another half smile. "I'll check my schedule and call you. Thanks for letting me come over."

"You never really said why you wanted to," Jean pointed out.

With her hand already on the doorknob, Lea turned back to her. "I wanted to see you," she said quietly. "Just to make sure you were okay."

"I'm okay," Jean said softly.

Lea leaned in and kissed Jean gently on the cheek. "I'm glad. Take care of yourself, Jean."

As she undressed for bed, Jean could still feel the warmth of Lea's lips against her cheek.

* * *

It was almost noon the next day before Detective Munson called Jean back. She explained about the missing file folders.

"Just a sec," Munson muttered into the phone. "Lemme get the—here it is. Inventory list. Um, yeah. Five manila file folders, in his briefcase. It was in the trunk of his car."

Jean felt a wave of relief. "Is there any chance I could borrow them?"

"Borrow them? I can't let you take them out of the inventory. They're evidence."

"I understand," Jean said, thinking quickly. "What if I came over to the station and looked at them?"

She could hear the reluctance in his hesitation. "I think it might be important to your investigation," she added.

"Uh, look, Ms. McAllister, I know you're a lawyer and all, but…"

Before he could finish refusing her, she took a chance. "Have you talked to Sheriff Hawkins today?"

"No." Now he sounded suspicious. "Why?"

"I think she'll vouch for my trustworthiness. Please schedule me for his afternoon, say around two thirty? I promise to stay out of your way. You can put me in an interview room or something."

Munson finally agreed but his reluctance was still clear in his voice. Jean was suddenly energetic. Surely there must be something in the file folders that would help them understand why Todd Moorman—and Fred Lambert—had been murdered.

She hadn't seen Del since her return from Dallas and she decided to check in. She considered telling him about her investigation into the murders and the connection with the Lambert file folders, but on the way down the hallway she decided to wait until she had turned up a firm lead.

Pacing on the carpet outside Del's corner office was Carolyn Forsythe. Jean greeted her and, gesturing to the closed office door, asked, "Is he with someone?"

Carolyn looked unsettled. She toyed with her gold bracelet. "I heard voices, but I hated to interrupt."

Jean looked surprised. Carolyn was Del's boss, at least one of them. Jean wondered why Carolyn would be reluctant to disturb him. Turning, Jean knocked firmly on the closed door.

A moment later the door was jerked open and she was face-to-face with an angry Del Franklin.

"What the hell is the matter with you, McAllister? Can't you see—"

Jean looked past him to see Commissioner Hayward Lyons standing behind Del. He looked even angrier than her boss did and Jean realized that she'd interrupted some serious disagreement between the two men.

"Never mind," Lyons said, spitting out the words. "I think we understand each other, Franklin."

He pushed past Del and Jean without apology and stalked down the hallway.

Carolyn was fluttering behind her. "Oh, Del, I'm sorry, Jean was just seeing if you were done yet."

Del glared at Jean but softened his tone for Carolyn. "Well, obviously not, since the door was shut. It's all right, Commissioner Forsythe. You know I always have time for you."

He ushered her in, turning briefly back to Jean. "I'm sure whatever you had can wait, McAllister." It was not phrased as a question.

"Just checking in," Jean said as calmly as she could. "If you need me I'll be in my office this morning. I have appointments out of the office this afternoon."

"Fine," he said brusquely, all but waving her away.

Good to see you, too, boss. Yes, my mother is recovering, thanks for asking. No, I'm not traumatized from finding my colleague murdered in the parking lot. Jean went back to her office in a sour mood, her energy of a few moments ago dissipated by Del's rude behavior. Why had she ever thought she would work well with Del Franklin?

The hell with him, at least for the moment. She returned to the never-ending river of work that flowed through her office.

CHAPTER ELEVEN

Detective Munson was wearing a blue blazer that looked like he'd owned it since his high school graduation. It was a couple of sizes too small, shiny at the elbows and when he crossed his arms to look down at Jean, sitting at the battered table in the interview room, she feared that the shoulder seams wouldn't stand the strain.

He laid the file folders, still in the heavy clear plastic evidence bag, onto the table's surface, avoiding the metal ring used to secure handcuffed suspects. "I had a talk with Sheriff Hawkins earlier today," he said, in his most lugubrious tone. "She seems to think very highly of your reliability and honesty. I gotta tell you, this isn't exactly regular procedure."

"I know and I do appreciate it," Jean said in her best mollifying tone. "I hope to be of some help."

He made a grumpy snort and left her alone. She wondered for a moment if he planned on watching her through the one-way window set into one wall of the room, but shrugged the thought away. Munson could observe her as much he wanted. All she was going to do was read.

Jean decided to attack the problem chronologically and pulled the pleadings file out first. She read everything, the Complaint, the county's answer, the various amended pleadings and motions. Everything seemed straightforward enough. Fred Lambert claimed that he'd been wrongfully terminated but the Complaint's allegations were vague, although that wasn't unusual. All the Complaint was required to do was put the other side on notice of the claim, not outline every bit of evidence the plaintiff had against the defendant.

The Motions to Dismiss and the Amended Answers didn't tell Jean anything helpful. She set aside the pleadings file and read the correspondence file next, the usual exchange of letters sparring over discovery details and haggling over dates. Del's general strategy for this case, at least, had been to raise every possible difficulty for the plaintiff and his attorneys. The more she read the more disgusted Jean became. Del was skirting the edge of proper ethical behavior without ever actually going over.

She shoved the folder aside and opened the bottle of water she'd brought with her. She needed to wash the taste of her boss's tactics out of her mouth.

The thickest files contained the discovery, the exchange of evidentiary information between the parties. The Interrogatories had been exchanged, written questions sent by one party to the other for answers. They helped define the issues and Jean read them closely. Lambert seemed to be claiming that his direct supervisor, a man named Bill Skelton, fired him because Lambert had complained about certain roadwork performed by the county for private citizens.

This was the first Jean had heard of the specifics of the allegations. She dug into the file until she found Skelton's deposition. He testified that Lambert was fired because he had falsified his time sheets and copies of the time sheets in question were endlessly discussed.

Jean finished the deposition no wiser than she'd been when she started. Several other public works employees were deposed, some claiming that Lambert was always at work when he was supposed to be, others supporting Skelton's version of events.

The conflicting testimony didn't surprise Jean. It always amazed her how much variation in the truth people could create.

She finished her water, surprised to see that it was after five o'clock. No one had disturbed her, but she supposed that a police station didn't keep regular office hours. Jean stretched, made a quick trip to the ladies' room, then returned to her little interview room. It was time to read Lambert's deposition and she didn't want to have to come back tomorrow.

The first sixty-three pages of the deposition covered Lambert's personal history and his twenty-two years of employment at the county public works department. Finally Del got down to the specifics of the whistle-blower claim.

Q: I am showing you your Interrogatory answer number seven, do you recognize it?

A: Yes.

Q: You claim that you were terminated because you complained about certain paving activities.

A: Not paving.

Q: Not paving?

A: No. It was grading operations on gravel roads. Private gravel roads, not paved.

Q: So you're claiming that you were ordered to grade private roads with county property?

A: I'm not claiming anything. I'm saying I was told to do work on private roads on county time.

Jean couldn't read intonation or hesitation from the pages of the deposition, but she could almost hear the disdain in Lambert's voice.

Del hammered Lambert about this claim for pages and pages. Jean shook her head. Del seemed to be trying to talk Lambert out of his statements instead of just pinning down the specifics of his testimony, the real purpose of the deposition. Arguing with the witness was the strategy of a mediocre lawyer.

Near the end, Lambert's attorney asked questions of his client to clarify the allegations.

Q: When did you perform these grading operations on the private roads?

A: In April and May of last year.

Q: And for whom did you perform these grading operations?

Franklin: Objection. The question is irrelevant to the issues in this case.

Q: Go ahead and answer the question.

Franklin: No, don't. I direct the witness to—

Q: Unless you're planning on calling the magistrate right now, my client is going to answer the question.

A: A lot of places. The road to Commissioner Forsythe's place out north of town. Deputy Treasurer Webb's house. The county clerk's brother, his house in Joya. And uh, Lou Hawkins's ranch, the sheriff's father.

* * *

The name "Hawkins" jumped off the page at her. Jean read the rest of the deposition in stunned disbelief. Lambert was claiming that his boss ordered him to do work on county time with county equipment for the private benefit of people with power.

People like Lou Hawkins.

Jean wanted to throw the deposition across the room or find the nearest shredder to destroy the ugly allegations page by page. If Lambert had been telling the truth, the motive was becoming clear. Lambert had been killed to prevent any further revelation about the misuse of county employees and county property. And Todd must have read the deposition and drawn the same conclusion, Jean realized. Todd had discovered the testimony from the deposition and that was when he must have called Jean. But the conspirators, whoever they were, somehow found out about it and killed him before he could talk.

What was she going to do? If she told Munson what she had discovered, she would involve Lea in a scandal involving her family. Jean couldn't imagine how devastated Lea would be to discover that her father had violated the public trust.

A chilling thought hit her. What if Lea already knew? What if she was the person who had asked public works to do the grading on Painted Horse Ranch? Or maybe Lea had discovered it after the fact and had helped cover for her father's corruption?

Jean couldn't believe it of Lea. It was almost as difficult to believe that Lou Hawkins would have cheated the public, but Jean didn't really know him. He certainly had plenty of powerful friends, so perhaps it was just a *quid pro quo* kind of favor. The thought made her slightly sick to her stomach.

Her cell phone rang. The caller ID read "Lea Hawkins."

Lea was calling about dinner. Jean couldn't talk to her. Not now. She had to think. She had to figure out what to do first.

She let the call go to her voice mail. She got two more calls from Lea that evening and she just stared at the phone lying on her coffee table. Jean wondered how long it would be before she could listen to the messages.

* * *

"We don't give out addresses of retired employees," said the officious voice on the other end of the line.

Jean hoped her sigh wasn't audible over the speaker phone. "Yes," she said calmly, "I understand the policy. I'm not asking you to release the information to the public. I told you I'm the deputy county attorney. I need Mr. Skelton's address because he's a witness on a pending lawsuit against the county. When did he retire?"

She could hear the clack of computer keys through the speaker. "That would be May 17 of this year."

Two weeks after his deposition testimony, Jean calculated. "Thank you. I do still need his current contact information."

"I'll have to transfer you to Ms. Jenkins. Please hold."

The human resources department head was more cooperative and a few moments later, Jean was calling Bill Skelton's new home phone number in Florida. If Lambert was telling the truth about the grading operations, then the falsified time sheets must have been a pretext for his termination. And that meant Bill

Skelton was lying. She wasn't sure how much she could get from him over the phone, but she'd have a difficult time explaining to Del Franklin that she needed to make a sudden trip to Palm Beach. Maybe now that he was retired, Skelton might be willing to tell her something that would help.

The telephone was answered on the third ring. "*Hola.*"

"*Buenas tardes,*" Jean tried out her college Spanish. "I'm calling for Mr. Skelton."

"*Señor Skelton no está aquí,*" the woman responded. House sitter? Housekeeper? Jean wondered. Between her basic Spanish and the woman's somewhat better English, she managed to discover that Señor Skelton was on an extended vacation in Puerto Rico. No, she didn't know when he'd be back. No, she didn't have a phone number for him.

Jean hung up in frustration. Outside her window she could see gray afternoon clouds building, glowering at the buildings below. Lea had told her that autumn was the season of afternoon rains, occasionally heavy cloudbursts that washed down the dry arroyos.

She called Ms. Jenkins in human resources again and found out the amount of Mr. Skelton's retirement checks. It was hard to believe that Skelton could afford an extended Caribbean vacation. Maybe he'd been saving up for it for a long time.

Or maybe, she thought cynically, someone had paid him off. Retire early and take a nice long vacation on us. Was it really worth all of this? she wondered. Payoffs and conspiracy and murder?

Who was behind this? Someone with power, with political pull. Almost unwillingly, she considered that it had to be an elected official. One of the board members? The treasurer, the county clerk? Or was it the sheriff?

It couldn't be Lea, she told herself. Even if Lea had stooped to cheating on county grading, she would never condone murder. At the same time, Jean knew how compromised her judgment was—her attraction to Lea rendered her far from objective. The thought that Lou Hawkins was involved was almost as uncomfortable. If he turned out to be involved somehow and Lea didn't know, telling her would be pretty terrible.

What was she going to do? She couldn't continue to avoid Lea forever. She couldn't think of a way to discover the truth behind the plot without Lea's help. Or could she?

Maybe Todd had done more work than she knew. Perhaps his notes on the case would reveal something that would help her. He might even have a draft memo to her on his computer somewhere.

A glance at her own computer confirmed that she was about to be late for a meeting with Purchasing about changes in the county bidding process. She'd have to return to this later and hope in the meantime to think of something to tell Lea Hawkins.

* * *

Jean was cleaning up her desk. It was nearing six o'clock and the rain had just begun to splatter on the sealed glass windows of her office.

Someone appeared in her doorway and Jean jumped in surprise.

"Sorry," Lea said quietly. "I didn't mean to startle you."

"It's okay." Jean sat down in her chair to recover herself. "I didn't expect to see you, that's all."

Lea moved into the office but stayed carefully away from coming too close. "You didn't return my calls."

Jean noticed it was a statement of fact rather than an accusation or an obvious attempt to make her feel guilty. Still, she picked up some sadness from Lea's eyes and she felt guilty anyway.

"You're right. I'm sorry," Jean said. "Things have been crazy."

Lea gripped the back of the visitor's chair but didn't try to sit down. "Is it your mother?"

Jean felt another stab of guilt. "No, she's doing as well as she can be."

Lea was looking at her closely and Jean had a strong sense of what it must be like to be a suspect subjected to her interrogation. Jean cleared her throat and said again, "I'm sorry."

"You don't need to apologize," Lea said. "Just tell me what's going on."

Jean felt trapped between the truth and her emotions. It had been such a long time since she felt that she could trust her feelings to guide her. Life with Charlotte, all the dramatic scenes of euphoria and despair, had destroyed her faith in her own judgment about other people. It finally occurred to her that this was another of the reasons she'd been so reluctant to become involved with Lea—or anyone else—since Charlotte's death. Somewhere she had lost her ability to trust herself to judge other people. She couldn't see their true motives, couldn't assess what they might be feeling or thinking. She couldn't meet Lea's gaze. It wouldn't help her to decide whether or not to trust Lea, she decided.

Jean spread her hands. "It's just work, a lot of stuff to do."

Lea's expression made it clear that she didn't believe Jean, but all she said was, "Okay. It's time for dinner and I think I owe you a meal. Or maybe you owe me one, I can't remember."

"Lea, I don't think—"

"Jean," Lea said more forcefully, "I think we need to have a talk and I missed lunch today. So unless you have other plans, I'd like it if you would come to dinner with me. All right?"

Jean was still torn. "Do you take no for an answer, Sheriff?"

Lea straightened. "Yes, I will take a no if that's really your answer. You told me once you weren't interested in a relationship with me and I will respect that. But I think you need a friend, Jean, and I'm offering my services, that's all."

Knowing how cynical she sounded, Jean said, "You really think you and I can be just friends?"

"Yes," Lea answered and Jean couldn't see any hint that Lea was being disingenuous. "Don't you?"

No, Jean admitted to herself. *I think about you all the time and I want you in my arms. Every minute I spend with you makes it worse.* Before reading Lambert's deposition she had been willing to take a chance on being with Lea, but now she couldn't risk it. Yet again she was unable to walk away.

"I don't know if we can be friends," she admitted. "But I would like some dinner."

Lea seemed to relax slightly and Jean realized how rigid her posture had been. "Okay, then. I know just the place."

* * *

"I admit it," Jean said as she unlocked the front door to her condo. "I've never eaten in a diner quite that good before."

"I like eating in local places," Lea said, coming in behind her. Jean noticed that Lea automatically glanced around every new room she entered. Searching for intruders? Or assessing the housekeeping skills of the occupant?

Jean chuckled to herself. Lea said dryly, "I could use a laugh. What's up?"

Conversation at dinner had been a tightrope walk between superficial commentary on everything from Jean's mother to Rita and Loren's evolving relationship to the weather and all the things Jean wanted to talk about but couldn't mention. Every instinct she still possessed told her Lea could be trusted, but did she believe in Lea? Did she believe in herself?

"I was thinking," Jean responded, "that I lack a natural homemaker's instinct. Even given my dereliction of housekeeping duties, would you like some coffee?"

"I'd love some." Lea sat at the counter while Jean dealt with the coffeemaker. "So you did enjoy the Blue Note?"

"I did," Jean admitted, happy to be on a safe topic. "I'd just assumed from the name that it was a jazz club."

Lea gave her a half smile. "Not much jazz in Tesóro, I'm afraid. The diner has been there as long as I can remember. Best french fries in town. My dad knows the owner pretty well."

At the mention of Lou Hawkins, Jean flinched. Lea caught the look. Hastily, Jean said, "How is it that you can eat hamburgers and french fries—and quesadillas—and still not gain weight?"

Lea sipped at her coffee. "I did manage to pick up about five pounds sometime after I turned forty that I can't seem to lose, but I've made my peace with it. As for the rest, I run and lift weights because in my opinion it's part of my job to keep fit. I just have a weak spot for junk food." After a moment, she added, "Now that I think of it, you're probably used to much better meals than pulled pork enchiladas at the Blue Note. I mean, since you were living with a chef and all."

Jean wasn't used to talking about Charlotte in a casual way, the way normal people discussed their ex-girlfriends. It actually felt good, as if she could acknowledge the parts of her relationship that made sense. She answered, "Actually, by the time she got home from work, Char was usually too burned out to make meals. She taught me a few basics and I did a lot of the cooking at home. I make a nice frittata. Leftovers are great to chop up and put in the eggs. And toast is another of my specialties."

Lea grinned, her first real smile of the evening. "Gourmet toast. You'll have to make that for me sometime."

Jean froze, the implication that she would be whipping up breakfast for Lea sometime unsettling her deeply. Lea said quickly, "I didn't mean—Jean, I'm sorry. If this is too hard for you, maybe you were right about us being friends."

Jean put her mug down on the tiled countertop, staring into the dark brown depths of the coffee. She desperately wanted a friend, but there was so much more that she wanted from Lea. Lea leaned across the counter and put her hand gently on Jean's arm. When Jean looked up, Lea said quietly, "Tell me what's wrong. Please."

Jean wanted to deny it, but instead she said, "I'm not ready to talk about it yet."

Lea studied her. "Is this something about Todd Moorman's murder? Did Munson let you read the files?"

Jean sighed. "I read the files. I have some more work to do before I'm ready to talk to you about it. All right?"

Releasing her touch on Jean's arm, Lea leaned back and said, "Yes. On one condition."

"What condition?" Jean asked warily.

"You cannot put yourself in harm's way," Lea said firmly. "Whatever it is you're working on, you've got to tell me—or Detective Munson—what you find. I don't want you playing amateur detective on this. Whatever's going on, somebody has killed two people over it. He or she or they are dangerous people. If you don't want to talk to me, talk to Hal Munson. But don't go off on your own. Okay?"

Jean wanted to resent her, but all she heard was the genuine concern in Lea's voice. Was Lea playing her, trying to find out what she knew to protect herself and her family? Or did Lea really care about her?

Jean was tired of questions, exhausted from trying to figure out what she should believe. What she wanted right now was to be in Lea's arms, and without thinking about it further, she went around the counter and stepped into Lea's embrace.

Lea opened her arms and folded them around her. For a moment, Jean just reveled in the warmth that seemed to penetrate her from Lea's embrace, but it wasn't enough. She brought her head up and kissed Lea.

She might have expected a hesitation from Lea because God knew Jean had been sending her mixed messages. But Lea kissed her as if they had been lovers for years, with passion and warmth and sweet desire. Jean stood next to Lea, still seated on the stool, and felt more heat from Lea's body than she'd ever experienced. Jean murmured, "I need you."

Lea pulled her in tighter, holding Jean firmly against her, her hands caressing Jean's back. They continued kissing until breathing became difficult for Jean.

"Lea, please," Jean said into her mouth.

To her dismay, Lea released her, although Jean could sense her reluctance. "Jean, what do you want?"

I thought that was pretty clear, Jean thought. Clearly I've lost my touch. "I want you to stay with me tonight," she answered, touching Lea's mouth with her fingertips.

"Jean, look at me," Lea urged. "I can't."

Jean felt faint shock. "Can't?"

"All right. I won't, not yet."

"Lea, what are you talking about?"

"You know I want this," Lea admitted. "I want you. But less than two weeks ago you were telling me why we couldn't have a relationship and now you want for us to become lovers. No matter how much I want you, I'm not going to stay tonight and then listen to you tell me tomorrow or next week that you can't make it work."

Jean said in frustration, "I can't give you guarantees."

"I don't need a guarantee, Jean. I need to know that you want to try to be together for more than a night. I won't settle for less. And I don't think you want to either."

Jean stepped away from the distracting circle of Lea's embrace. "I'm pretty sure you don't really know what I want."

Lea squeezed Jean's hand once then released it. "Maybe not. But please think about what I've said. When you're ready to talk about this again, we'll talk. Okay?"

After Lea had gone, Jean dumped the rest of her coffee down the sink. Her frustration was aimed almost equally at Lea and herself. Lea had led her on and then rejected her, or so it seemed. Yet Jean understood how mixed her own emotions were. She'd been ready to go to bed with Lea without even being certain that Lea could be trusted.

Jean realized that her head was pounding. Not tonight dear, she thought ruefully, I have a headache. She took herself sadly to bed alone.

CHAPTER TWELVE

On Wednesday morning, Jean's day started with a call on her cell phone from Maryke. "Hey, you," Jean said. "What's up?"

"First things first," Maryke responded. "How's your mother?"

Jean gave her as much detail as she could of the news she was receiving daily about her mother's rehabilitation. "Ron's been great," Jean finished. "I think he's actually happy for the first time because she needs him."

"And she's not able to drink," Maryke added cynically.

"There is that," Jean conceded. "How's your current boyfriend?"

"Things are going well. Of course, I have traded in the one I told you about last week for a newer model."

"Of legal age, I trust."

"I checked his driver's license at the bedroom door. And since we're on the topic of romance, how's the local sheriff?"

Jean grimaced. "Well, we did go to dinner last night."

"And?" Maryke asked suggestively. "Did we manage some lesbian loving?"

"No," Jean admitted. "Just some making out."

"Wait. You were making out with her and you didn't make the main attraction? Jeez, I thought you ladies jumped into bed at the slightest provocation. It's not like you can get knocked up or have to run out to the drugstore for a package of Trojans."

"You don't know what you're talking about," Jean snapped at Maryke, her temper flaring hot. "Responsible lesbians practice safe sex and we do not 'jump into bed at the slightest provocation.'"

"Okay, all right. Jesus, Jean, I'm sorry. I've never heard you go off on me like that."

Jean rubbed her temples, hoping last night's headache wasn't about to make a return appearance. "Look, things are just a little jumbled up for me right now. Work, Mother and everything with Lea is complicated."

"Well, you already know my advice to you about the sheriff is to uncomplicate it. You have to give her a chance, Jean."

"It's not that simple. Look, did you call me just to harass me about my love life?"

"Doesn't sound like much of a love life to me," Maryke retorted. "But actually I called to give you some good news. Is your computer on, I assume?"

Maryke gave her a website and within moments Jean was watching the video she'd taken of her brother ranting outside their mother's hospital room, with identifying information about his congregation affiliation predominately displayed. Maryke had enhanced the audio and done some video effects including closeups of Bobby's florid face.

"Oh, my God!" Jean laughed into the phone. "Wait until someone in his church sees this."

"I don't have to wait," Maryke chuckled. "I managed to locate a handy church directory complete with email addresses for Bobby's congregation. At this very moment various members of his Sunday school class are enjoying this clip along with their morning coffee breaks. I can also imagine his pastor is getting a few calls about it as he's preparing next week's sermon. Hope he's enjoying the extra publicity for his church."

"You are a crazy woman, you know that? What if Bobby decides to sue for defamation?"

"Oh, pooh, stop going all lawyer on me. He'll never sue, he'll just want to run away like all bullies do when they're confronted. And if he does sue, I'll be very pleased to hire a publicist and make his life even more miserable."

"You did all this for me?" Jean was touched, her earlier anger dissipated.

"Only partially. Mostly I did it because Bobby's a twenty-four carat jerk and he deserved it. So enjoy and let me know if there's any fallout. And take my advice, Jean. Give your sheriff a chance, will you?"

If only it were as simple as that, Jean thought as she punched off her phone.

A glance at her schedule reminded her that she had a deposition on a case involving an accident on a county road set for all of the next day. Whatever work she could do in Todd Moorman's office would have to wait until Friday unless she could get it done today.

Her opportunity came after lunch. Rita, her designated lookout, told her Del Franklin had left for the day. Jean told Rita to keep an eye out as she prepared to go through Todd's office. She didn't want to have to explain to her boss what she was doing, at least not yet.

"What are you looking for?" Rita asked her. "Can I help?"

Jean considered. "Todd didn't give you anything in the last few days before he died, did he? Notes or correspondence, anything?"

"No, nothing. Is that what you're looking for?"

"Yes," Jean admitted. "But I don't even know if what I'm looking for exists. Wish me luck."

"Good luck. Is it important, what you're looking for?"

"Maybe," Jean responded. Maybe it got Todd killed.

She'd been through Todd's office before, but she'd been searching specifically for the Lambert file. Now she was looking for something much harder to find because she didn't know what form it might be in.

Jean tried Todd's file folders first, since she thought it was at least possible that he'd made a file on the Lambert case. She found no such file, so she next went through every drawer in his desk and credenza, looking for handwritten notes. All she discovered were blank legal pads. Many had been used, but the remaining pages were blank. She found not a single written note anywhere.

That left his computer. Jean found a couple of thumb drives in his desk drawer, so she powered up his computer and began to go through the files on the drives. Nothing seemed promising until she found a single file labeled "lambertmemo."

She opened the file, relieved that it wasn't password protected. It was a draft of a memo Todd had written to her about the Lambert case. She checked the date—it was dated the morning of the day Todd had died.

The first paragraph contained the usual summary of the assignment she'd given him, then discussed his efforts to perform research on the case. She read the last paragraph.

> It appears that the plaintiff Lambert's claims that he was terminated for his knowledge of improper use of county resources for private purposes are unsupported by the available evidence. Such claims may have been fabricated by the plaintiff to justify his...

The draft ended in mid-sentence and Jean frowned at it. She couldn't remember the last time she'd left a memo like that, even in a first draft. Had Todd been interrupted while he was writing? Or perhaps another thought had struck him and he'd left off, thinking to get back to it at a later time that never arrived.

She finished her search but found no other reference to Lambert's case. Disappointment mounted as she logged off Todd's computer. Outside the office she could hear the low chatter of voices and clacking of someone typing at a computer keyboard. She was no closer to the answers than she had been two hours ago. Sighing in frustration, she returned to her own office.

How was she going to find out about Lou Hawkins if she couldn't even prove whether or not Lambert was telling the truth? Although logic told her that if Lambert had been lying as Todd's memo suggested, he and Todd would still be alive. There was no reason to kill them unless there was a cover-up.

Why hadn't she followed up with Todd earlier? Jean berated herself. She might have saved his life. Or, she considered, she might have been one of the victims as well. She remembered Lea's warning of the night before.

Her cell phone rang and Lea's name appeared on the display. She smiled at the coincidence and answered, "Were your ears burning?"

"All the time," Lea responded. "Were you talking about me?"

"Only to myself," Jean said.

"That sounds interesting," Lea said and Jean could hear the smile in her voice. "Listen, I know this is really short notice but I wondered if you were free for dinner tonight."

"After last night, I thought you might wait more than eighteen hours to ask me out again."

"Technically, it's not my invitation. My mother is very insistent that you make an appearance at the ranch tonight. Apparently Loren has invited Rita over for dinner and Mother wants another friendly face at the table. You've been elected to act as a buffer. Are you up to the job?"

Jean considered the level of discomfort she might have if she had dinner with Lou and Linda Hawkins. But her next thought was that she might be able to find out from Lea's family what she couldn't discover otherwise. It seemed worth the chance.

"I'll be there," she said. "What time?"

* * *

"All I'm saying," Lou Hawkins pointed his fork at his son, "is that horses will always have a place as working animals. I don't care how many ATVs you've got, there's terrain that will always require a horse. And there are parts of the world where horses are pretty much all there will ever be for everyday transportation."

Loren chewed and shook his head at the same time. "What century are you living in? There's hardly anyplace where you can't hear the sound of an engine, from the Arctic to the Amazon jungle."

Lea shot Jean a look across the table. She muttered, "I'm so glad we're going to be treated to the latest version of this argument."

"They've had this one before?" Rita interjected as she finished off the last bite of her cherry pie.

Lea said, "Every dinner since Loren was old enough to sit at the table and talk."

"There may be engines, but horses can go where vehicles can't, you know that," Lou continued. "That's why there'll always be a need for them."

"That's nuts," Loren argued. "Soon there won't be anywhere a vehicle can't go. People keep horses because they want to, not because they have to."

"That's not true everywhere," Lou said forcefully. "Can you imagine rounding up cattle with a bunch of Jeeps? I'm saying—"

"Good God, Dad, nobody does round-ups. That's what feed lots are for."

Linda Hawkins asked brightly, "Anyone need more pie? There's plenty left."

Lou said, "I'll have some more."

"That question was not directed at you, dear," Linda responded sweetly. "Loren, more pie?"

"Why does he get seconds?" Lou grumbled. "I work as hard around here as he does."

"His last cholesterol reading wasn't through the roof," Linda answered. "Would anyone like more coffee?"

"I'll get it," Lea offered. She refilled Rita's cup and Jean's as well. "That was a wonderful meal, Mrs. Hawkins," Rita said politely.

"Thank you. We're so glad you could come this evening." Her smile around the table included Jean and Lea as she added, "You know how much I love having my children and their friends come to the ranch."

Loren said to Lea, "Don't you love it when she refers to us as the children?"

"I feel so young," Lea laughed.

Jean turned to Rita and said, "Just wait until you get invited back for the chili."

Now everyone laughed, Linda included. Loren turned to Rita and said, "Are you up for an after-dinner walk? Or would you like to go see the horses?"

"Oh! I'd love to see the horses," Rita answered happily. "Do you think we could bring Jay out sometime? I'd love for him to see them too."

"Sure thing," Loren said and it pleased Jean to hear the happiness in his voice.

Lou added, "You and your boy are welcome anytime, Rita. Has he ever ridden?"

"No. We've just never had a chance to do that."

"Why don't we find a time over the weekend for you two to come out? I think we could spare Loren for a couple of hours."

Rita curled her fingers around Loren's arm. "That would be just great."

Loren beamed. "Let's go pick out a nice horse for him, honey."

After they had gone, Lou said to his wife, "Well, that seems to be going well."

"Lou, leave them be. It's still new for them." She gave Lea a lifted eyebrow.

Lea cleared her throat and said, "I'll load the dishwasher. Why don't you guys go into the living room?"

Jean rose. "I'll help you."

"No, it'll only take me a minute. Go on."

It suited Jean's purposes to have a private conversation with Lea's parents, so she let Lea clear the table alone and followed the Hawkinses into their living room, carrying her coffee cup.

Here goes nothing, Jean thought, gathering her courage. If she concentrated on how much was at stake in the next few minutes, she knew she wouldn't be able to go through with the conversation.

"The flowers still look great," she began.

Linda said, "Thank you. The rains will keep them fresh for a while."

"Yes. Lea told me the rainy season is just about here." After a moment she added, "She also said it can wash away a lot of the gravel roads. Yours seem to be in really good shape. I noticed them driving in. Do you grade them yourselves?"

She held her breath and for a moment she thought there would be no response. Then Linda said, with mock severity, "My dear Jean, you're not allowed to mention our roads."

"I, ah, what?" Jean fumbled.

Lou growled, an incoherent noise.

"Lou, leave her alone," Linda said. "We shouldn't talk about it. Your blood pressure, dear."

"My cholesterol, my blood pressure," he groused. "Leave me alone, woman."

Linda rolled her eyes. "Oh, don't call me woman, old man."

"I hate to interrupt," Jean said carefully, "but what's the big problem with the roads?" She was trying not to shake and she had to set her coffee cup down on the table beside the sofa.

Linda answered her. "Some silly mix-up year before last that had Lou spitting nails. A county public works crew came out and graded all of the roads on the ranch."

"A county crew? You mean a contractor?" Jean tried not to sound disingenuous.

"No," Lou snorted, "county equipment and employees. Can you believe that?"

Oh, yes, Jean mused. I can believe it, all right. Aloud she said, "Well, you don't need a lawyer to tell you how illegal that was."

"You're quite right, young lady, I do not," Lou Hawkins grunted. "And let me tell you, when I got home, I had a few phone calls to make. And Linda's right, I was madder than a hornet's nest."

"I'm guessing you didn't know anything about it ahead of time, then," Jean said.

"Hell, no! I got some supervisor on the phone—who was it, Linda?"

"A Mr. Skelton."

"Yes, Skelton, that's right. His story was that his crew thought it was a county-maintained road. That was nonsense and I told him so. I finally had to talk to Hayward Lyons. He assured me the people responsible would be disciplined."

"Commissioner Lyons told you that?"

"Well, he wasn't a commissioner at the time. He was still the head of public works. But he said it was a misunderstanding and he'd take care of it."

Well, it got taken care of, Jean thought. Skelton got early retirement and an all-expense-paid trip to Puerto Rico and Fred Lambert got fired—and then murdered. Was Lyons the one behind this? Or had he been told what to do by whoever was really responsible?

At least one thing was clear to her: Lou Hawkins was telling the truth. The indignation was still in his voice and on his face and Jean believed every word he was saying. She said, "Did you tell Lea about this?"

Linda interjected, "We didn't want to bother Lea. Lou didn't tell her for months and when he did, she was none too happy about it either. But it was over by then."

Apparently not. But Jean was convinced by his fierce reaction, and so relieved that Lea and her family were innocent of wrongdoing that she could barely keep track of the rest of the conversation.

Lea came into the room, wiping her hands on a dishtowel. "Everything's squared away, Mom. What are we talking about in here?"

"Nothing interesting," Jean answered. Her voice sounded so bright that Lea gave her an inquiring look. She switched the subject by turning to Lou and saying, "So tell me all about paint horses. How do you get the colors you want in the animal?"

Lou Hawkins happily delivered a long discussion of American quarter horses, Thoroughbreds and the difference between paint horses and pintos. By the time he finally wound down, Linda was openly yawning.

"Time for the old folks to go to bed," Linda said. "Come on, Lou."

"I suppose my bedtime is doctor's orders too," he grumbled, but he got to his feet. He took Jean's hand in both of his big rough ones and said, "Don't pay us any mind. You're welcome to stay as long as you want. Anyone who survives two meals in the Hawkins household is officially family."

After they had gone, Lea said, "Are you all right? You've been jumpy all evening."

Jean, aware that Loren and Rita could return to the house at any moment, responded, "How would you feel about sitting out on the porch for a spell?"

That got her the wry grin from Lea. "I don't know how long a 'spell' is, but I'm happy to have a chat on the porch."

They settled onto the bench in front of the house. The dogs appeared from wherever they'd been to join them, lying happily within reach in case some friendly human felt inclined to pet them.

The faint breeze was warm and carried the sweet and spicy scents of sage and juniper to Jean's nose. Night air caressed her skin, the perfect warm temperature to relax her. There were no sounds of traffic here, no city lights to blind them. The night sky was velvet black, with a generous jeweler's display of diamond stars strewn carelessly across it. Jean could feel herself relax, the cold knot of fear that had tied her down for days finally easing.

Lea said quietly, "Will you explain something to me?"

"If I can."

"First I think you might be attracted to me and then you tell me you don't want a relationship, that you can't be with anyone. Yet you seem to still be interested in me. I don't know how to feel. I don't know what to do. Do you want me to leave you alone? Try to be your friend? Convince you that I care about you and that I still want more? Tell me what's going on with you, Jean."

Jean sighed. "It's complicated."

"Yes," Lea said dryly. "I figured out that much for myself."

"It has to do with Todd Moorman's murder, my friend Maryke and my mother."

Lea settled back and propped her boots on the porch railing. "I think I'd better get comfortable. Sounds like this could take a while."

Jean started from her trip to Dallas to see her mother to her conversation with Maryke to her return and the news about Todd.

"I was ready to call you and invite you out to tell you I'd changed my mind about dating," Jean admitted. "But then I read Lambert's deposition, trying to find a reason Todd might have been killed. And that's when I discovered…" Her voice trailed off. How exactly was she going to tell Lea she believed her father was crooked?

"Just say whatever it is," Lea said.

A single coyote howled somewhere in the foothills far away. The sound of loneliness.

Jean explained about the deposition and what Lambert had said. Halfway through the story, Lea took her boots off the railing and planted her feet on the wooden planks of the porch. Jean finished by saying, "I still don't know what happened, but your father was so upset, even after all this time, that it's clear to me that he had no idea about the county grading his roads."

Lea was quiet for a long time. Jean wondered what she was feeling.

"I knew it wasn't a mistake," Lea said at last. "Dad was angry that someone would think he'd exercised his influence to use county equipment for his private benefit, but he always thought it was just some mix-up. Now I know it wasn't an error—either someone was trying to do him a favor they could collect on later or maybe they were trying to get some influence over him."

"Extortion, you mean?" Jean hadn't thought of that.

"Maybe." Lea shrugged. "Whatever the reason, I have to think it's connected to Lambert's murder. My investigators are convinced that Crabtree, our Joya burglar, had nothing to do with Lambert's death. And I'm still convinced that Lambert's murder is connected to Moorman's death as well."

"Your father said he talked to Hayward Lyons," Jean said. "You think he was responsible?"

"I don't know. He was probably just following orders from someone else, since he was just a county department head at the time."

"So the question remains: who was responsible?"

Lea exhaled a long breath. "I have a bad feeling that whoever it is, he—or she—is a very highly placed county official."

It was a disturbing thought, one Jean had already had. Probably only an elected official would have the power to manipulate the county resources or issue orders to Hayward Lyons. "How are we going to figure this out? I've been through Todd's office but I can't find anything that indicates what his research might have turned up. Other than the deposition of Fred Lambert, of course."

Lea looked thoughtful. "I'll run some background checks, see if I can turn up anything personal or financial in anyone's background that might be a motive. Maybe I can find something on Lyons that we can use to pressure him to tell us what he knows. Assuming he knows anything."

"How many elected officials are there? That could take a while."

"Yep. I'll try to prioritize." She gave her typical half smile. "I imagine I can leave the investigation on the sheriff for last."

"Good thinking." Jean grinned back. "If I can do anything else, let me know."

"You've done quite a bit," Lea responded. "And I'll remind you that we've had this discussion before. I don't want you doing anything remotely dangerous. Okay?"

"Okay," Jean agreed. "I'm not interested in putting myself in the line of fire. I'll leave that to professionals. People who carry guns."

"Don't forget it," Lea said emphatically. "Now, how about we talk about something else?"

Jean felt happy and relieved. "Sure. What do you want to talk about?"

She could feel Lea's gaze on her in the shadows. Warmth began to seep into her belly, then slide lower into her body.

Lea said, "We're really going to have a relationship, right?"

"Yes, please," Jean murmured.

"Good. Come here."

Jean moved closer, expecting a kiss. But Lea gently turned Jean in her arms so that she was holding Jean comfortably against her side. "What are we doing? Not that I mind," Jean added.

Lea put her mouth close to Jean's ear. "I have a meeting tomorrow night," she began. "And I was planning on going into the office on Saturday afternoon to catch up on some work, so I'll be downtown. I'm free Saturday night if you are."

Jean felt a pleasant shudder run through her. "Do you want to come to dinner? I'll make something easy. A casserole."

"Um hmm," Lea said softly. "I'll bring wine."

"That sounds nice."

Lea shifted a little closer to Jean. "I want to make you happy. Tell me how, Jean."

Jean was amused. "You want to sit on your parents' porch and talk about having sex? What are we, fifteen?"

Lea laughed too. "At fifteen the only sex I was having was in my imagination."

"Anyone in particular?"

"Yes, actually," Lea admitted. "Cheerleader at our basketball games. Her name was Shasta as I remember. Legs up to her neck."

"Shasta? Isn't that a cola?"

"You're funny. What about you?"

"At fifteen, I was learning all about French kissing from Stacy Miller."

"Sounds like fun. But I was hoping to get farther than first base on Saturday night."

"I can't believe we're actually talking about this in advance," Jean said.

Lea nuzzled her hair. "Why not? Good sex is mostly about what happens in our heads anyway. I like to think about it for a while, don't you?"

If she thought about it any more, Jean thought, she'd have to explain why she was taking her clothes off on the Hawkins's front porch. "I do, actually," she admitted. "I—"

"Tell me," Lea said in a voice that made Jean's bones melt.

"I like to take my time," Jean murmured at last. "Go slowly, I guess."

"I'm a very patient woman," Lea whispered and Jean began to seriously consider whether she could get them both naked before anyone found them.

"God, Lea, come home with me," Jean urged.

Lea kissed her temple. "Not tonight. Go home and dream about us together. Think about me when you're at work tomorrow. By Saturday it'll be wonderful. I'll make it good for you, Jean, I promise."

"What about you?" Jean asked. "Unless you don't want me to."

Lea's arms tightened around Jean, the warmth from her body penetrating through Jean's skin. "You want to know what will really get me going?" Lea said. "Making love to you. That's all I'll need. By the time you touch me, I'll—"

Jean pulled Lea down to her mouth and kissed her hard. Long moments after, Lea said, "A couple more minutes of that and we're not waiting until Saturday."

Jean nipped at Lea's neck. "Okay by me."

"Are you going to behave or not?"

"Not."

"Then you," Lea said as she got to her feet and pulled Jean up with her, "have to go home now."

Jean tried her best pout. "Don't want to."

"Come on. It's a school night. I'll call you at the office tomorrow when I get a minute."

They walked out to Jean's car. Jean could smell the faint scent of rain on the air for the first time in a long while. Behind them the dogs got up, stretched and ambled out with them like a canine body guard.

Lea got Jean settled and shut the car door behind her. Leaning down, Lea said, "Do me a favor? Call me when you get home. I want to know you're there safely. Okay?"

"All right." Jean found Lea's courting style of her a little old-fashioned, but deeply charming. She drove back to the condo dreaming happily of Saturday night.

CHAPTER THIRTEEN

Lea's hands were on her shoulders, the long strong fingers caressing Jean's bare flesh. Jean could see the dark flecks in Lea's eyes, feel Lea's breath against her cheek.

"Jean?"

They moved together, skin against skin. Heat penetrated Jean to her core and Lea moved her hands down to—

"Ms. McAllister?" This time the voice jolted her out of the daydream. She'd been staring out the window, not seeing the splatters of rain against the glass. She fumbled for her glasses that were lying on her desktop.

"Yes? Sorry, Rita. I was thinking about something."

"You looked a million miles away."

Jean got her glasses on and managed a smile. "Something like that. What's up?"

Rita stepped into the room and lowered her voice a bit. "I wanted to thank you for coming last night. I think Loren was really nervous about me meeting his parents and it was nice of you and Sheriff Hawkins to be there."

"It was not a problem," Jean said. "Linda's a great cook. And by the way, I think Lea told you to stop calling her Sheriff Hawkins."

Rita's complexion reddened. "Well, yes, but we're at work. She seems really nice. She always seemed kind of scary to me before."

"Yes," Jean had to agree. "She can be pretty scary I think, if she wants to be. But she is a really compassionate, kind woman."

"Um. Can I ask you a question? If it's too personal, you can tell me and I'll go away."

Jean thought she knew where this was going. "All right."

"Are you...um, are you and Sheriff Hawkins...I mean, at dinner it kind of seemed like you might be...together."

"Rita, I'm happy to tell you but for the moment I'd appreciate it if you would keep it confidential. Yes, Lea and I are dating, but I need to talk to Del before things progress much further. I haven't had a chance to do that yet, so please don't tell anyone, okay?"

Rita seemed relieved. "Of course not. Loren thought maybe you were going out, but I didn't want to assume. Thanks for telling me. I promise to keep it to myself until you tell me it's all right."

Jean leaned back in her desk chair. "And are you and Loren getting along well?"

Now Rita was blushing dark red. "He asked me to go away with him next weekend. Jay can stay with his grandmother and he and I can, um, get to know each other."

Jean grinned at her. "That's fantastic, Rita. I'm so happy for you."

"Me too. I mean, I'm happy for me too, but I meant I'm happy about you and Sheriff Hawkins. Loren told me she's been really great to him, that she takes real good care of him and their parents. He kept talking about how he hoped she could find somebody again. Apparently he didn't much care for her last girlfriend."

"Really?" Jean's curiosity as usual got the better of her discretion. "Did he say why?"

Rita was clearly eager to discuss the subject further. "He said the family only met her a few times even though they were together for years. He said Lea almost always saw her only on the weekends and that he never thought she was nearly good enough for his sister." Rita gave Jean a happy smile. "He likes you a lot better."

Jean returned the smile. "Glad to hear it. I'll try not to mess it up, then."

Rita said, "I really came in here to ask you if you need anything. I mean, you asked me about Todd's notes and I didn't know if you found anything."

Sighing, Jean admitted she'd been unsuccessful. "I'm still not sure whether or not there's anything for me to find, anyway. But if anybody says anything about Todd or any of his cases, let me know, okay? I'm still not sure why Todd was killed, but it might be connected to work."

Rita looked thoughtful for a moment. "I did have a question this morning about him, now that I think of it."

"Really? From whom?"

"Commissioner Forsythe. She came over to see Mr. Franklin, but he wasn't here. When I told her that, she asked me an odd question. She asked me if I'd heard anything from Todd's wife."

"Heard anything? Like what?"

"She didn't say. I just thought that was peculiar."

Jean agreed. She couldn't think of a reason why Carolyn Forsythe would care one way or the other. "Did she go back to her office, do you know?"

"I think so."

Jean decided she needed to have a brief chat with Commissioner Forsythe. After a few minutes of rummaging around, she located a memo she could use as an excuse to go make the visit.

Carolyn Forsythe was sitting at her desk, staring out her window as Jean had been doing a few minutes earlier. Jean was pretty certain that her thoughts, whatever they might be, were quite different from Jean's daydreams.

She handed Carolyn the memo and managed to discuss it convincingly for a few moments. Carolyn seemed troubled, so at last Jean asked, "Excuse me for asking, Commissioner, but you seem a little distracted. Is there anything I can do?"

Carolyn had a gold pen in one hand and she was drawing circles on a lined yellow pad. At first Jean thought she was going to deny any problem, but Carolyn seemed to change her mind. She answered, "How well did you know Todd Moorman?"

Interesting opening, Jean thought. She responded, "Only as a co-worker. He was a hard worker, I know."

"Did he leave a family? I know he had a wife."

"I don't believe they had children. Someone told me they'd only been married a little over a year."

"Oh." She seemed simultaneously relieved and more disturbed. "Almost newlyweds, then."

Jean remembered the brief mention Todd had made of his wife. He had seemed far from a man besotted with love. "I guess so."

"Such a senseless death," Carolyn continued.

"Yes," Jean agreed, watching her carefully. "Just for a car."

Carolyn appeared to be surprised. "That's right, I'd forgotten. A carjacking. And they didn't even get the car."

"No." The vision of Todd lying in his car swam before her eyes for a moment. Jean realized again that she had never quite bought the carjacking theory. Why wouldn't the car have been taken? How long would it have taken to shove Todd out of the car and drive away? The killer could have been miles away long before the police arrived. No, it had to be an intentional shooting, not random. Frustration rose again. Why couldn't she track down what Todd had been doing?

As she left Commissioner Forsythe's office, she ran into Jaime Fontana, the board's chairman. He seemed to have used even more Brylcream this morning, his black hair gleaming like onyx under the fluorescent lights in the hallway.

"Ms. McAllister," he greeted her. "How are things going in the county attorney's office?"

She wondered why he didn't ask Del Franklin. Maybe he just couldn't think of anything else to say to her. "It's challenging," Jean answered him. "It's difficult to lose a colleague, especially so suddenly. And as you know, we're not a large office, so we really feel shorthanded as well."

"Yes." He sounded distracted. "Well, there's a budget for outside counsel. Del could certainly use that to hire some extra help if you need it."

"That's a good point," Jean agreed, wondering again why she was having this conversation with him. "I'll discuss that with him when I have a chance."

"Good, good." He rubbed his hands together and proceeded down the hall, already moving on to his next problem. She thought perhaps he was the kind of politician who only paid attention to people he needed.

Later in the afternoon she was able to complete her trifecta of conversations with the board members when Hayward Lyons appeared in her doorway.

"Commissioner, what can I do for you?" Jean asked politely.

He jerked his head toward Rita's desk. "No one seems to know where Del is," he complained. "Did he tell you where he was going?"

"I'm afraid I haven't seen him today," Jean said. "Is there anything I can help you with?"

"No," Lyons answered abruptly and turned away.

The county building was just filled with charming politicians today. How on earth did these people win popular elections?

The high point of the day was the promised phone call from Lea. Jean smiled at the caller ID and said, "There you are. Busy day, I guess."

"Hi." Lea's warm voice cheered her even more. "Yep, they're all busy these days, it seems like. How is your day going?"

Jean snuggled back into her desk chair. Just talking to Lea made her feel young again, a time when love was an adventure to be anticipated rather than a trial to be endured. "A weird day but fine," she answered. "No chance to do anything else in Todd's office today."

"Don't," Lea said. "As I told you before, you should let the professionals handle the case. We're still running some background checks but it'll take a while. Whoever is behind this has killed two men and we don't need any more potential victims getting involved."

"Are you always this bossy?"

Lea cleared her throat and Jean could hear the half smile in her voice. "Not always," Lea said softly. "Only when it counts."

Jean felt a warm tremor run through her. "Stop that. I've already been having enough trouble concentrating on work as it is."

"Oh, yeah? Any particular reason?"

"Stop fishing for compliments, Sheriff. I'll discuss this with you tomorrow. Unless your plans have changed for tonight," she finished with hope in her tone.

"Afraid not," Lea said sadly. "But we'll have dinner tomorrow, come hell or high water, all right? I've gotta go, but if you're up for a late-night conversation, I'll call you when I get home tonight. It'll probably be pretty late."

"Gosh, whatever will we think of to talk about late at night all alone in our own beds?" Jean asked.

"Now who's being distracting?" Lea laughed. "I'm trying to drive here and you're discussing dirty late-night phone calls."

"I said no such thing," Jean protested.

"Save the denial, Counselor. You want prurient discussion after midnight you'll get it, all right."

"Prurient? Did you store up that word for a special occasion?"

"I was saving it just for you. Told you I like smart girls."

"Stop talking now," Jean sighed. "I'm going to go back to work and try very hard not to think about you any more. Goodbye."

Jean managed not to think about Lea more often than every other minute for the rest of the workday.

* * *

Saturday morning was bright and warm, but from her western windows Jean could see clouds building over the mountains. She was full of energy from last night's telephone talk with Lea, which fulfilled its promise for prurient content.

Now Jean attacked the condominium with mop and dust cloth, cleaning and shining while the washing machine thrummed with a load of sheets and towels. Once the bed was remade and the fresh towels hung up in the bathroom, Jean found herself with nothing left to polish.

She assembled the casserole, layering tortillas with chicken, cheese, onions, peppers and enchilada sauce. It would take a while to bake this evening and she could have a glass of wine with Lea while it cooked.

She took a shower and spent a pleasant few minutes debating what to wear. Jeans and a blouse with the matching black bra and panties, she thought, casual on the outside and a little naughty underneath. Then, restless, she decided to go into the office until Lea was ready to come over.

The clouds that had been fluffy white that morning were now darker, their flat bottoms crowding the sky in a threatening canopy of gray. The usually dry air smelled of the coming rain and Jean welcomed the thought of the dinner she would share with Lea, the two of them snug in the condo against the showers outside. It had been so long since she'd been with a woman she hoped she hadn't forgotten what to do. Jean laughed at herself as she pressed the elevator button. She was pretty sure it would all come back to her quickly.

Jean cleared her desk of everything she could do on a Saturday afternoon. She drafted routine letters and reassigned work to the paralegals. The pile of professional journals still crouched on her credenza, trying to lure her into catching up on her reading but she resisted. The connection between the Lambert case and Todd Moorman's murder seemed obvious to her and she wished she'd found something in Todd's office to help Lea and Detective Munson.

One more try, she said to herself. She went down the hall and into Todd's office.

She'd searched every file and every drawer of Todd's desk and examined his computer files. What else could she look for? Opening his desk drawer, Jean spotted Todd's card with his Westlaw number and password printed on it. Like most attorneys, he kept it handy for his frequent logins to the computer-assisted legal research database. Westlaw permitted the researcher to enter a word or phrase as search terms and then designate the specific database to be searched. State or federal statutes were popular choices, but the most frequent use of the database was to find relevant case law from a specific jurisdiction. The long, grinding task of looking up case law in multivolume digests had been replaced with a few keystrokes. Jean knew the trick was determining what search terms to enter. Getting the right phrase to produce the desired result could take several tries.

An idea struck her. Jean turned on Todd's computer and logged onto his Westlaw account. On the home page was the tab she remembered: "Last Research Trail." The tab permitted the user to resume research without having to reenter the search terms. She clicked on the link and read the page as it loaded.

The search term Todd had last entered appeared in the box and got Jean's full attention. "Malfeasance Committed Prior to Taking Office." It didn't make immediate sense to her but she looked at the list of cases the term had pulled up. She clicked on the links to the Colorado case law one by one and scanned the case reports themselves.

An hour later she sat back in the chair. A grumble of thunder outside the office windows caught her attention for a moment and she noticed a few splatters against the glass. The rain was beginning gently but her mind returned to everything she had just read.

In researching case law concerning liability of public officials for wrongful acts committed prior to taking office, Todd had uncovered one notable case involving a state elected official who had committed tax fraud prior to his election. Because the fraud hadn't been discovered until after he had taken office, the case discussed whether the official could be removed for acts that predated his election.

Jean realized that it didn't matter what the ruling in the cases had been. The fact that Todd had been researching them told her everything she needed to know about who was behind the murders. Jean hit the print key on the page with the search term and she heard the printer in the copy room across the hall begin to spit out the pages.

Fred Lambert had given up the key fact in his deposition without being aware of it and it had gotten him murdered. When Todd had discovered the reference, he had disregarded it at first, as his draft memo indicated. Then he must have had second thoughts, Jean realized, and begun this line of research.

She reached for the telephone and punched in Lea's cell phone number.

"Hi," Lea answered. "I'm almost finished here. Are you at the office?"

"Yes. Lea, I know who killed Lambert and Moorman. Or at least who ordered it done."

She'd been an idiot, she realized. The killer had an accomplice, someone who knew what had happened and had protected the conspiracy at every turn. She didn't know why yet, but it had to have been—

Del Franklin stood in the doorway of the office. She looked at his florid face for a moment before her gaze dropped involuntarily to his hands. One hand held the pages she'd just printed out. The other hand held a gun. She gripped the receiver so hard her fingers hurt.

"Say goodbye and hang up right now," Franklin said. "Don't say another word." He lifted the barrel of the gun a fraction of an inch for emphasis.

Jean managed to choke out, "I have to go now. Goodbye." Then she punched a button on the phone and slowly replaced the receiver.

"Del," she said, "why are you pointing a gun at me?" She was amazed at how calm her voice sounded.

"I never should have hired you," Del said through gritted teeth. "Goddamn nosy bitch. You couldn't just mind your own fucking business."

"Are you the one who killed Fred Lambert and tried to make it look like it was the burglar?" Jean asked.

"This is not a damn television show, McAllister. I'm not going to stand here and explain everything to you. Where is the file?"

"What file?" How long could she play for time before he got impatient and just shot her?

Franklin took a step forward and raised the gun again. His face was brick red, the veins in his forehead prominent as ropes. But his expression was cold. "I'm done fucking around with you. I told Rita to shred the file and she obviously screwed up. Now where are the *fucking* folders?"

She tried to think of an answer that would help her but after a moment settled for responding with the truth. "The Tesóro Police Department has them. That's where I read them, at the police station."

"God *damn* it to hell," he snarled. He was close enough now that Jean could see sweat glistening at his hairline. "All right, get up. We're going for a walk."

"No," Jean answered immediately. "I'm not going anywhere with you, Del."

He shifted suddenly to her side of the desk and put the gun hard against her head. "If I have to I'll blow your brains out right here. It'll be a tragic suicide."

Jean wanted to laugh hysterically. Of all the deaths he could arrange for her, surely an apparent suicide would be too ironic to bear.

How long had it been since he'd come into the office? One minute? Two? Her fear was making the time elongate grotesquely.

"Where are we going?" she asked. Delay, delay.

"Just a little walk," Franklin said. "I just need for you to stay put for a while until I get out of here. I won't hurt you unless you make me."

She didn't believe a word of it, but she needed more time. "Tell me where we're going."

"Upstairs," he answered, jabbing her again with the gun. "Now move."

He pushed her ahead of him, grabbing her arm and steering her toward the stairs. The county attorney's offices were already on the eighth floor and the only floor above them was the one housing the commissioners' offices and meeting rooms. Were they going to meet Franklin's boss? But they passed the door to that floor on the stairwell, so they must be headed to the roof.

Was there a place for him to lock her in? No, he must be intending to shoot her outside the building on the roof, a place where no one would see them. Perhaps he was going to wait for some thunder to mask the gunshot.

Franklin had no hope of getting away, but it didn't help her to know that. For all the awful days after Charlotte's death she had wished she were dead too, today she desperately wanted to live. How long could she delay him? How long would be long enough?

Jean let herself slip on a stair, stumbling to her knees. Franklin dragged her up, wrenching her arm and sending pain shooting into her shoulder. "Clumsy bitch. Move!"

She could hear the tension in his voice, thin and taut as a piano wire. He pushed her through the door marked Roof and she stumbled again, genuinely this time. Franklin let her fall and she waited a moment on her hands and knees, trying to catch her breath. Think, try to think.

Cold raindrops splattered onto the back of her blouse, just a few but with the promise of a deluge soon. Franklin barked, "Stand up."

Jean got to her feet and looked around. The roof had a parapet about as high as Jean's waist, topped with a single metal railing. There were a couple of structures, HVAC systems, she guessed, but nothing that looked like a storage shed. He was going to shoot her. She was going to die on this stupid roof before she could reclaim her life. Before she and Lea had even begun.

In desperation she lunged at him, trying to wrestle the gun away. He jerked back in surprise, momentarily losing his balance as she clutched at his wrist. She pushed the weapon away, but with his free arm he slugged her clumsily in the face.

Her glasses smashed into her nose then flew away. He punched her again and Jean went down, still maintaining her hands on the sleeve of his jacket.

Franklin swung a heavy leg into her and Jean crumpled in pain as he caught her in the side. She waited for the next blow. The one that would finish her. The one from a bullet.

Instead he was dragging her across the roof. The asphalt was scraping at her and she could feel blood streaming from the bridge of her nose.

They hit something. He was dragging her up, trying to get her onto her feet. Why? She was dazed, but she continued to scrabble for his arm.

"Motherfucker," she heard him mutter.

The next moment there was a hard rod across her stomach. He was bending her over and for a wild moment she thought he was going to rape her. Then she felt her center of gravity begin to shift forward. Into nothingness.

He was going to throw her off the roof.

Terror gave her strength. Jean twisted, facing him. He continued to push at her, the metal railing now crushed against her back.

"No!" she screamed at him. Her grasping fingers found the front of his shirt and she clutched at him like an anchor. Rain was coming down harder and his face was wet and slick. His eyes bulged, his breath was rasping and hard on her cheek.

"This is the sheriff!" She barely heard the yell above the crack of thunder. "Franklin, stop now!"

Oh, thank God! Lea was here. Jean couldn't see her, but Lea's voice rang out again.

"I'm warning you, Franklin. Let her go or I'll shoot!"

She saw no hesitation in his face. Oh, my God, Jean thought in all-out panic. He hadn't heard Lea over the storm.

She tried to scream at him but all her breath was taken away by struggling to keep her balance. She still couldn't see Lea. She couldn't see anything but Del's face contorted in desperate rage, blurred by the pounding rain.

Where was Lea? Jean feared she couldn't fire her gun at them because Jean was locked in Franklin's hold at the edge of the roof. She fought frantically.

Franklin got one leg up on the edge of the parapet to increase his leverage

"Fucking bitch!" he bellowed and pushed Jean over the edge.

She tightened her grip on him in horror. She felt him fall toward her.

They both went over together.

At the last instant she let go of him, flailing out with both arms for anything to grasp. One hand caught something cold and hard.

When she realized she wasn't falling through space Jean fought to get her other arm onto the railing. She finally managed it, but something heavy was pulling her down toward oblivion. Her body felt impossibly heavy, twice its weight.

Below her she heard screaming. It was Del, hanging on to her, wrapped around her legs, dragging her down toward death.

The railing was slick with rain. She wasn't going to be able to hold on for more than another second or two.

Then Lea was there, her hands strong on Jean's wrists. Her voice rang clearly over the pounding rain pouring into Jean's face.

"I have you!" Lea called. "Hold on, for God's sake!"

"I can't," Jean groaned. "I can't!"

"Hold on!" Lea yelled again. She leaned out over the railing, her body nearly over the edge.

Jean screamed, "Let go, Lea! We'll pull you over!"

She felt the release of Lea's hands on her arms and knew that Lea was going to let loose of her and let them fall. Jean tried to look up into the stream of rain flooding over her. She wanted Lea's face to be the last thing she saw.

She felt an icy circle of steel against one wrist. Lea snapped the other end of the handcuff onto the railing and folded Jean's fingers around it.

"Hold on," Lea said again, the words harsh in her throat.

Lea slid over and leaned out even more. "Franklin!" she yelled. "Give me your hand!"

Her fingers of one hand slipped off the wet metal. Jean cried out, scrambling to regain her hold. The metal of the handcuff bit into her wrist.

The pain in her shoulders was agonizing. Jean screamed as she felt Franklin shift, crawling up her body. Lea loomed over them with one arm stretched out to grab at him.

"Give me your hand!" Lea called out again.

A flash of lightning tore through the sky. Jean felt another shift, then a blessed release of the weight dragging her down. For a moment she thought Lea had him, but the next instant she heard the scream echoing up from the alley below her, piercing through the sharp crash of thunder.

Her arms felt wrenched half out of their sockets. Jean managed to lift one hand up to the railing into Lea's grasp.

"I've got you!" Lea gasped.

She pulled Jean up, wrestling her over the metal railing. Jean sprawled on the rough asphalt trying to ground herself back into the world.

Dimly she was aware of Lea releasing the handcuff. Jean's arms ached, her face hurt, her ribs were sore. But she welcomed the pain because it reminded her keenly that she was alive.

Jean leaned back and realized Lea was sitting on the roof behind her, holding her. The rain was freezing cold on her skin but Lea's arms encircled her, strong and warm.

"I've got you," Lea repeated. "It's okay, I've got you."

* * *

Jean couldn't get her fingers to work well enough to get her key into the lock of her condo. Lea leaned over and gently took it from her. She unlocked and opened the door.

"I'm sorry," Jean said. "My hands are just so cold."

"I should have made you go to the hospital," Lea said. "I'm not sure the paramedics checked you out enough."

"I'll be fine once I warm up." Jean shut the door behind them and went wearily into the kitchen. "I'm thinking we're not up for the casserole tonight."

Lea followed her. "Go sit down. I'll make coffee, it'll help warm you. You're really sure you don't want to go to the emergency room?"

Jean sagged limply onto the couch in the living room. "I'm sure. My shoulders are sore, but there's not much they can do for that. Everything else is just minor. God, I'm just freezing."

In a minute Lea brought her coffee, steam rising from the mug. "Drink this," Lea urged her. "In a second I'll go run a hot bath for you. A good soak will help too."

Jean wrapped her fingers around the mug, drawing the heat into her bones. The first taste of the hot, bitter coffee rolled through her warmly.

The evening was surreal to her, the sharp edges of her memories smudged by the few minutes of stark terror on the roof.

Franklin had fallen nine stories to his death. The red emergency lights had pulsed in the alley for what seemed like hours, glistening on the rain-soaked pavement in garish tones. Jean had looked down from the roof at the broken doll of Franklin's body before the police covered him.

Officers in uniforms and officers in plain clothes had asked endless questions of her and of Lea as well. Jean wondered how much longer it would have taken them to get home if Lea hadn't been the sheriff.

The Tesóro police finally let them go. Jean couldn't drive home safely without her glasses, so Lea got her truck and took them back. During the short ride home she and Lea hadn't talked, but Lea had held Jean's hand tightly all the way to her door.

Jean looked up to see Lea watching her with a frown creasing her forehead. "I'm all right," Jean said.

"I'm sorry," Lea said quietly. "I was almost too late."

"Oh, God, Lea." Jean reached over and grasped her hand. "You saved my life."

"You saved yourself. Franklin had no idea you put the phone call to me on speaker?"

Jean shook her head. "I was afraid you'd say something, but it was all I could think of to do. You must have run all the way."

"I was crazy to get to you," Lea answered and Jean realized for the first time how terrified Lea must have been.

Jean put her coffee cup down and went into Lea's embrace. Lea tightened her arms around her and Jean said, "I'm sorry you were scared."

"I thought I was going to lose you," Lea whispered.

Jean smiled a little. "For a minute there, I thought you had too," she answered.

Lea stroked her hand slowly down Jean's back. "How did you figure out the accomplice was Franklin?" she asked.

"It had to be," Jean said. "He told Rita to destroy the Lambert file. And he tried to keep Lambert from testifying about the people Lambert did the grading roadwork for at the deposition. I should have put it together sooner." She lifted her head and met Lea's eyes. "I wasn't doing something stupid, Lea. I just couldn't stop wondering what the connection was."

"Okay," Lea said, kissing her temple. "It's okay."

"I just can't believe he killed Todd too," Jean continued. "Do you think you'll be able to prove it?"

"I think there's at least a fifty-fifty chance he used the same gun to shoot Lambert and Todd and that it's the one we found on his body. When we verify that, we'll get an arrest warrant for his boss."

The memory of the cold metal barrel of the gun against her head made her shudder. Lea said, "Let's not talk about this any more tonight. Go take off your wet clothes and I'll run you that bath."

Jean stripped off in the laundry room to put her clothes in the dryer, sadly removing the black underwear she'd put on that morning in happy anticipation. Lea hadn't given her any indication that she would be staying tonight and Jean knew they couldn't recapture the anticipation they had shared. But her body was humming with yearning. She suspected it was the aftermath from the terrors of the evening but all she could think about was the way Lea's arms felt around her as she stepped into her robe.

In the bathroom. Lea was sitting on the side of the bathtub, holding her hand under the water running from the tap. "Almost ready," Lea said.

Jean crossed the room and turned off the water. "I don't want a bath," she said.

She heard Lea's breath catch. "Then what do you want?"

"You," Jean answered. "I want you."

Lea stood and moved next to Jean, so close but without touching her. "Jean, you went through something awful. We don't have to do anything just because you feel, I don't know, grateful or scared or—"

Jean took off her robe and let it drop to the floor. She watched Lea's face transform into something wonderful, filled with a fierce desire.

"Lea, please," Jean said.

Lea took Jean in her arms and kissed her with slow, heated deliberation. Jean said against her mouth, "Now, now."

Lea backed Jean up against the vanity. Jean was desperate for her touch and she demanded Lea's passion with urgent pleading. She trembled in Lea's intimate embrace, warmth inundating her body with pleasure. Lea held her upright as her climax ebbed.

"Jean," Lea murmured in the quiet, her hand soft between Jean's thighs. Lea buried her face into the gentle curve of her neck.

Legs trembling, Jean murmured, "Come to bed with me."

Lea drew back and Jean saw uncertainty in her eyes. Jean smiled. "Oh, we're just getting started."

* * *

Jean lay on her clean sheets and watched Lea as she undressed. Lea had her eyes on Jean's face and Jean smiled at her. Lea gave her the crooked smile that turned Jean's heart over. She could see how relaxed Lea was in her own body and it made her even more attractive. She said, "You have no idea how much I want you."

"This isn't what I'd call going slowly."

"So we'll just have to try again."

Lea came to her and said softly, "Tell me what you want, Jean. Show me."

She asked all of the questions silently, one by one.

Here? Or here?

More?

Like this?

And Jean answered every question with her body, gave up the secrets of a lover to Lea. She surrendered everything. When she finally had to beg Lea to stop, Lea collapsed happily on top of her. Jean cradled Lea's head on her belly, stroking her fingers through the soft waves of her hair.

"All right?" Lea asked softly.

"God, Lea."

"I'll take that as a yes. Sleep if you can. I'll be right here."

A pleasant heaviness rendered Jean nearly immobile. "Will you hold me?"

She could feel Lea's smile on her skin. "As long as you want."

With Lea's arms securely around her, Jean drifted into the soft clouds.

Not drifting, falling. She was falling into nothingness. Her body tensed as she waited to hit the ground.

"No!" She jerked awake, then sat up, trembling. A dream, it was only a dream.

The next moment Lea was holding her shoulders, caressing her as if she were gentling a horse.

"It's okay, Jean. You're safe. I'm here."

"Sorry," Jean murmured. "Nightmare."

"I'd be more surprised if you didn't have one. What can I do?"

Jean's shoulders ached. "How about two ibuprofen and some water?"

Lea brought her the pills and a glass. Jean swallowed the medicine and said, "Thanks. Sorry I woke you up."

"I wasn't really sleeping. I was listening to you breathe."

"Sounds kind of boring."

"It wasn't, actually. I'm just so grateful—" She stopped and Jean realized she was close to tears.

Jean turned and said, "Come here."

Lea seemed to dissolve into Jean's arms. Every part of her was smooth and strong, yielding, inviting. Jean explored her, taking pleasure in her pleasure, surprised and delighted at Lea's easy submission.

Finally Lea gasped, "Touch me now."

Jean took her over the edge joyously. As Lea sank back down into the bed, she clutched at Jean. Jean's head found Lea's shoulder and she circled one arm around Lea.

"Thank you," Jean whispered.

"I think I'm supposed to say that," Lea replied, her voice thick and drowsy.

"Will you stay tonight?" Jean asked softly.

"As long as you want," Lea answered a moment before she relaxed into sleep.

CHAPTER FOURTEEN

Jean woke to the pleasant aroma of freshly brewed coffee. She sat up and stretched. Her shoulders were painful and a gentle probing of her side revealed a darkening bruise. Her nose was sore too. She groped for her glasses before she remembered they lay smashed on the roof of the county building. She finally found her backup pair in the bedside table drawer.

The memory of the fear came back to her, but it was at arm's length now, softened and eased by the night in Lea's arms. She didn't know where they were going exactly but she would always be grateful that Lea had been with her when Jean needed her.

Lea came in looking freshly showered. "Good morning," Lea said. "How do you feel?"

Jean gave her a full report. Lea handed her a steaming mug and gently touched Jean's cheek. "You're going to be looking a little like a raccoon, I'm afraid. I should have put ice on that last night."

Jean sipped at the hot coffee and warmth curled into her stomach. "We were busy last night."

The halfsmile appeared on Lea's face. "We were too busy to have dinner, in fact. You must be starving."

Jean eyed her, disappointed that Lea was wearing the robe Jean had discarded on the bathroom floor. "I'm hungry, all right. Come back to bed."

"Before you've finished your coffee? What a loose woman you are."

"You have no idea. Come here."

Lea sighed deeply. "I really, really want to. But I have to go. I have a lot of work to do today and I have to get ready for a press conference we're doing live for the noon news."

"On a Sunday?"

Lea's face became grim. "We watched the county attorney fall off the roof of a building last night while he was attempting to kill his deputy. We haven't had a news story this big in years. I need to tell the press some of what we know while we make sure Franklin's boss doesn't get away."

"Are you going to make an arrest today?"

Shaking her head, Lea responded, "Not unless we have to. Tesóro PD is watching the house just in case. I want the ballistics report on Franklin's gun first and we're going to execute search warrants today on both home and office."

Jean absorbed this. "You're going to be gone all day, I guess. Do you need me?"

Lea leaned in for a kiss. "I sure do."

Jean returned the kiss and murmured, "I mean at the press conference."

Lea sat back again, clearly reluctant. "No. In fact, I recommend you stay in all day. The press and God knows who else will be calling you. If I were you, I wouldn't answer the phone unless you know the number. Just hide out at home and recover a little. There will be lots of time for you to face people tomorrow."

"Okay." Jean added a moment later, "I'm sorry you can't stay. We could have breakfast, read the Sunday paper and just loaf around."

"I promise you such a Sunday morning in the near future."

Jean chewed at her lip. "So you're not going to suddenly become too busy to see me again?"

Lea took the mug from Jean's hand and put it on the bedside table. She put her hands on either side of Jean's face, holding her firmly and looking into her eyes. "Jean, last night was better than I imagined it would be and believe me I thought it was going to be pretty wonderful. I think you're beautiful and giving and sexy as hell. I would like nothing better than to stay with you today, but I really do have to go. I'll call you later, okay?"

Lea's words warmed her down to her toes. "Okay. Go be the sheriff for a while. Will I see you tonight?"

"Well, I don't know. Is the casserole still available?"

"Absolutely."

"I'll be here. I don't know how late, but I'll be here."

* * *

Jean watched the news conference on television. Lea had changed into her uniform and looked so cool under the reporters' questions that Jean had trouble remembering the warm and passionate woman in her bed last night.

Lea said that official identification of the body was "pending notification of next of kin." She would only identify the body as "a county employee" and hinted that the official investigation hadn't yet determined whether the death was a homicide, suicide or accident.

Jean shook her head. It had been an accident, in a way. Certainly Del had had no intention of dying. The thought caused her to realize with a jolt that she hadn't thought of Charlotte once yesterday, not at the moment she thought she was going to die nor when she was making love with Lea. She really had put Char behind her, she realized. She had finally left Charlotte in her past where she belonged.

Did she have a future with Lea? She hoped so but Jean still wondered. They were apparently highly compatible in bed at least, but there was so much more to know. As she watched Lea, she realized that being with a law enforcement officer was probably always going to be difficult. Late-night calls and huge volumes of work—never mind the challenge of Lea being an elected official—faced them if they decided to continue their relationship.

She set her uncertainty aside for the moment and turned off the set. She had turned her cell phone off before her shower but now she picked it up and checked her voice mail.

There was a brief message of concern from Rita and a much longer one from Linda Hawkins. She jotted down both numbers to return the calls. She didn't bother to note the numbers of the two newspapers, three television stations and one radio station that wanted to interview her about last night. But there was also one call she felt compelled to return right away.

"Commissioner Forsythe," Jean said. "Thank you for calling."

"Oh, my dear," Forsythe sounded genuinely distressed, "are you all right? I just talked to Carl Parson at the *Tesóro Press* and he told me all about it."

I doubt that, given what Lea isn't telling the press. Jean said cautiously, "I'm not sure what he told you."

"He said—he said it was Del—I can't believe it, I just can't believe it. It must be a mistake of some sort."

Jean bristled. "I was there, Commissioner and I can promise you that Del Franklin managed to throw me off that roof."

"Oh! Of course, I didn't mean it—I didn't mean you'd made a mistake, I just—why would Del do such a thing?"

Jean didn't want to risk saying anything more, so she settled for, "He didn't tell me. I'm sure the police and the sheriff's office will figure out everything eventually."

"Yes, of course. Of course. I should call Jaime and Hayward again, I suppose. We'll need to write a press release or something tomorrow. You'll be there, I assume?"

"Why?" Jean exclaimed. Then she remembered: the board met with the county attorney every Monday morning at ten o'clock. "Is the board making me the acting county attorney?"

"Yes, of course. I talked to Jaime and Hayward earlier this morning. Who else? I mean you haven't been here all that long but you're Del's deputy after all. And whatever else is going on, we at least know you're not involved."

Jean wanted to laugh. How fortunate it was that she'd been a victim of Del's murder attempt. She didn't want to think what this would mean for her relationship with Lea. She said, "We can talk about this in the morning, Commissioner. I'll see you then."

She related the conversation to Lea over their late dinner that evening. Lea had arrived looking tired and Jean tried to guide the conversation away from her day until they were settled with coffee cups in her living room.

"I talked to your mother today for a while," Jean said. "She called to find out if I was all right. It took all I had to keep her from driving over here to give me chicken soup and a shoulder massage."

Lea smiled. "That's Mother. I'm surprised she didn't ask for details about last night."

"Are you referring to Del Franklin trying to kill me or what happened after we came home?"

Lea came close to spewing her coffee. "Holy hell, you didn't tell her about—"

Laughing, Jean said, "Well, of course. She's your mother, so I figured she'd want to know every detail."

Lea glared at her. "You had better be kidding."

"I'm kidding."

"Thank God," Lea sighed. "All I need is one of her 'advice' sessions on how to treat a girlfriend."

"Wait. Maybe I want to hear more about this."

"You don't, believe me. How about another topic? Any other topic."

"Can you tell me about what you found today?" Jean asked.

Lea set her cup down. Jean was beginning to recognize an air of quiet satisfaction when Lea was pleased about her work. "It's been an expensive day for the city. Lots of overtime, but it was all worth it. Ballistics matched on the gun in Franklin's pocket. He killed Lambert and Todd Moorman as well, we're pretty certain. But the interesting thing is the motive."

"How did you figure that out?"

Lea shook her head. "Notes on his home computer. Fortunately he was the kind of man who wrote his password down in his desk drawer. Apparently he was planning to run for office."

"Del? What office?"

"Perhaps not surprisingly, county commissioner. He wanted to replace Fontana when his term was up in two years. There were notes about funding and campaign strategies."

"Two years in advance seems awfully early."

"Not these days. It seems clear that everything he was doing was in an attempt to get as much support for his election bid as possible. That certainly made him easy to manipulate."

"Commissioner Forsythe called me this afternoon. A reporter told her about Del."

Lea sighed. "I'm not surprised. I called in enough favors to keep the news from being official until tomorrow, but it's hard to keep a secret like this. It's the crime story of the decade here."

Jean thought for a moment. "Did you get the arrest warrant?"

"Judge issued it late this afternoon. It's sealed, of course. We thought we'd serve it tomorrow. We still have a team watching the house just in case."

"I'm meeting with the board at ten a.m. It seems I'm the new acting county attorney. What about the meeting as a time and place for you to make the arrest?"

Lea frowned. "I'm not entirely sure I want you anywhere near this arrest."

Jean reached over and stroked the back of Lea's hand. "I understand how you feel, I do," she said quietly. "But I really would like to be there. I think I'm owed a moment of satisfaction after last night."

Lea nodded reluctantly. "All right." She moved down the couch and curled herself around Jean. "Don't ever do that to me again, okay? I've been in law enforcement for almost twenty-five years and I've never been as terrified as I was last night."

Easing her hands down Lea's back, Jean responded, "Won't it be like that for me if we're together? Won't I worry every time you walk out the door, wondering if you'll come home?"

Lea went very still. "I don't know. Jean, if you can't handle what I do, I don't know where that leaves us."

Touching Lea reignited all of her feelings from the night before. Jean answered, "I hope it leaves us together tonight. Or do you have to go home?"

"I do have to go home later," Lea admitted. "But not just yet. Did you have something in mind?"

"Yes," Jean said. "But I'd rather show you than tell you."

Lea gave her the crooked smile. "I'm really fine with that."

CHAPTER FIFTEEN

Jean walked into the board meeting room at exactly ten o'clock. As usual, the three commissioners were seated in the chairs facing the western view. The mountains looked scrubbed clean from the recent rains, bright purple-blue against the sky. Jean herself felt new and refreshed. Lea had had to leave before dawn but every hour before that had been a joy. The proof that their first night together hadn't been just an accident or the aftermath of her near-death experience cheered Jean immensely.

"Good morning," she said to the three commissioners. The tension was so strong that it felt like another person in the room with them. Carolyn Forsythe had her bejeweled hands busy with a pen, worrying it endlessly from one set of fingers to the other. Jaime Fontana looked tired and his shaving that morning left much to be desired—there were a number of dark whiskers visible under the line of his jaw. By contrast, Hayward Lyons looked preternaturally still, like a waiting predator. Jean went around the table to take a seat, grateful that she would be the only one facing the door.

"How are you holding up, Ms. McAllister?" Commissioner Fontana asked.

Jean was well aware that her face looked like she'd been in a prizefight that she'd lost badly. Her shoulders were still painful, but she'd been able to lift her arms to wash her hair this morning so she deemed that an improvement. Fortunately Lea had demonstrated that everything else on her body seemed to be working quite well.

"I'm fine," she said briskly. "It's been a difficult weekend, as you might imagine."

"Yes, certainly. We do appreciate your dedication, coming in to work this morning."

"Commissioner Forsythe indicated to me yesterday that our first order of business this morning is a press release," Jean said.

Carolyn interjected, "We thought we should make an official statement. Trying to make sure that we express the appropriate amount of regret without assuming any undue responsibility for Del—Mr. Franklin's actions."

Politics, Jean sighed inwardly. Corruption, extortion, murder and they're worried about public relations. She looked across the table at Hayward Lyons and his hatchet-thin face. He was glaring at her although he hadn't said a word.

The door opened and all three commissioners turned in surprise. Lea came in first in full uniform, with Detective Munson following as close as her shadow. Two uniformed officers from the Tesóro PD hovered in the doorway behind them.

"Sheriff, we're in a meeting here. Please leave," Fontana demanded.

Carolyn Forsythe rose to her feet, shaking. "What on earth is going on here?"

Lea ignored them both. "Hayward Lyons, we have a warrant for your arrest. Please stand up and put your hands on your head."

"What the hell!" Fontana exclaimed. Forsythe sank down into her chair again, all color drained from her face.

"Ward, what are they talking about?" she asked, her voice trembling.

Lyons turned and glared at her. "Shut the hell up. Christ."

Munson reached up and put handcuffs on Lyons. As he shifted him away from the table, Lyons said to Lea, "This is bullshit."

"There are two counts of conspiracy to commit murder and one of attempted murder. I think you'll be interested to know that the late Mr. Franklin had quite a bit to say about you in his personal notes."

"Notes from a dead man!" Lyons spat.

Jean realized how much he had been counting on Franklin's death to keep him safe. From his perspective it must have been just as good as Jean falling to her death instead.

Munson marched Lyons out of the room, saying over his shoulder, "Sorry to break up the meeting, folks."

Jean wanted to laugh—Munson had actually made sort of a joke. She didn't think he'd had it in him.

Lea was the last to leave the room, making brief reassuring eye contact with Jean before she left.

Jean cleared her throat. "I think it's time we started to work on that press release," she said to the two stunned people remaining. "We have a lot to cover."

* * *

Jean pushed back from the Hawkins's dinner table, leaving half of her enormous T-bone untouched on her plate. "What I don't understand," she said, "is why every one of you doesn't weigh four hundred pounds."

Linda Hawkins was busy stacking plates. She rescued the leftover steak from Jean's platter and said, "Everything gets worked off on the ranch. I'll save this for Loren's lunch tomorrow."

"Loren?" Lou complained. "I eat lunch here too, you know."

Linda smiled sweetly and said, "Yes, I'm aware of that. I have some nice fresh tomato salad for you. I saw your last cholesterol numbers, remember dear?"

Lea laughed at her father's scowl and he pointed a finger at her. "Don't you be so smart, young lady," Lou said. "She'll be starting in on you next."

"My cholesterol is just fine, thanks," Lea retorted.

"That's not what I meant," Lou grunted.

"Uh-oh," Lea muttered, rolling her eyes.

Jean looked from Lou to Lea to a still-smiling Linda. "Shall I ask what's going on or not?"

"I'd say not," Lou said. "What I want to hear about is what happened with Hayward Lyons. Did he confess?"

Lea sat back in her chair and took a long drink of water. "Pretty much," she began. "Although Del Franklin's death gave him a chance to shift as much blame as possible."

Linda sat down again at the table, the plates forgotten. "What did he say, Lea?"

"It all started when Lyons was still the department head over at county public works. He was doing free road grading with county equipment as a 'favor' to certain individuals, as he put it. Sadly, but maybe not surprisingly, Dad is the only one who ever called to complain about it. The district attorney is having kittens trying to decide if he has enough to go to a grand jury for half-a-dozen indictments against various county employees and elected officials."

"It would serve 'em right," Lou declared.

"Yep," Lea agreed. "But it probably won't happen. There's no proof they asked for the grading, any more than you did, so it'll be tough to prove a corrupt motive on their part. Lyons, on the other hand, was just doing everything he could to get elected as a county commissioner. And it worked."

"But what I don't understand," Linda interjected, "is why he had to murder two people. This all happened months and months ago, didn't it?"

Lea nodded. "The problem was Fred Lambert. He didn't know about Lyons's plan, he just did what he was told. When he got sideways with his boss and got fired, he sued the county and was using the lawsuit to threaten Lyons with his knowledge of the illegal work. Apparently Lyons tried threats and money to get Lambert to back off, but we think Lambert wanted more than Lyons was willing to pay. Lambert just had no idea how far Lyons would go to protect himself."

Jean shook her head. "I can never understand why people use murder to cover up lesser crimes. It makes no sense to me."

"It's not logical," Lea agreed, "but people do it a lot, believe me. They really convince themselves that they won't get caught if they just kill a witness."

"So how was Franklin tied up in all this?" Lou asked.

"He wanted to replace Jaime Fontana and he had been very busy getting in Carolyn Forsythe's good graces. Flirting with Carolyn was working, but since flirting with Hayward Lyons wasn't going to work, Del basically agreed to do Lyons's dirty work. Lyons claims Franklin came to him, which I don't believe for a minute."

Lou snorted. "Okay, I get how getting the two sitting commissioners on his side would help him get the party's nomination, but honestly, how stupid can a man get? Lyons did all that for a job as a county commissioner? Christ, it doesn't pay that much."

Lea shrugged. "Apparently after a lot of years as a county employee, Lyons wanted to run the show. He figured he'd be elected chair as soon as Jaime Fontana was termed out. But Del Franklin had higher ambitions, according to Lyons, anyway. Franklin wanted to be governor someday, but he figured he needed a track record as an elected official at the local level first. Lyons told us that Del planned next to run for the general assembly. Lambert was in his way, as was Todd Moorman once he figured out what was going on."

"Poor Todd," Jean said sadly. "When he couldn't get me on the phone that Friday evening, he apparently went to Del and told him what he'd found."

Lea nodded. "Lyons insists that Franklin killed Moorman on his own initiative and didn't tell Lyons until after the fact. That may or may not be true. It's hard to prove one way or another. But either way, Del pulled the trigger."

"But I keep wondering, if Carolyn Forsythe was innocent," Jean said, "then why was she asking about Todd's wife? She's been acting jumpy as a cat the last few days."

"Interviewing her was interesting," Lea replied. "In the end, she admitted she suspected that something was up. Franklin was acting squirrelly and he apparently kept mentioning Moorman to her."

"Maybe he felt guilty," Linda said quietly.

Lea lifted an eyebrow, the one with the faint scar over it. "If he did, it didn't stop him from throwing Jean off the damn roof, now did it?" Her tone was acid.

Jean reached over impulsively and took Lea's hand. "Lea, it's done. He certainly paid for it."

Lea took a deep breath and blew it out. "You're right. Lyons is looking at counts of conspiracy to commit murder, accessory after the fact and conspiracy on the attempted murder charge, not to mention charges for corruption of a public official. He'll be in prison for a long, long time, I imagine."

"Well," Linda said. "He certainly should be. And now before someone changes the subject again," she glared at her husband, "I would like to ask another question."

"Here it comes," Lea murmured.

Linda looked pointedly at Jean's hand, still intertwined with Lea's on the tabletop. "I was wondering if perhaps my daughter had some news for us."

"Gosh, Mother, whatever could you mean?" Lea asked in her best innocent tone.

Jean couldn't keep from laughing out loud. "Oh, my God. Is she always like this?"

"Yes," Lea and her father answered in unison.

"I prefer to think of it," Linda said with an air of dignity, "as a caring concern for my children's lives. Now that Loren and Rita seem to be off to a good start on a new relationship, I thought perhaps Lea might have a similarly happy situation."

"You want to take the Fifth?" Jean asked Lea. "You can lawyer up now. I'm here."

"Nope, I'll confess. Yes, Mother, Ms. McAllister and I have decided that we are officially going steady. Are you happy now?"

To Jean's surprise, Linda jumped up and came around the table to her, leaning down and hugging Lea, then her. "Oh, my dears, yes! Very happy."

Was this what it was like to have a family? Jean thought. It felt like nothing she'd ever had before, not with Charlotte or her own mother and brother.

Lou Hawkins produced a bottle of champagne from the kitchen somewhere and even Jean drank half a glass. Finally Lea said to her parents, "With your permission, I would now like to drive my sweetheart home before it gets too late."

They escaped, but not without more hugs and a few happy tears from Linda. When they were in Lea's truck, Jean said, "Good grief. What do they do when somebody gets engaged?"

"Depends," Lea answered, driving slowly down the gravel road. "If Mother approves, as she did with my older brother, you get a very large barbeque. If she does not, as in Loren's first marriage, you get a tight-lipped 'Congratulations.'"

"I see. Do you think we're in line for the barbeque someday?"

"Honey, you got champagne for going steady. I clearly underestimated how much my mother wants me settled down. If her reaction tonight is any guide, we'll probably get a weekend-long ranch party complete with a side of beef and a rodeo."

Jean smiled at the thought. "Where are we going, by the way?"

"I thought nine thirty was a little early for turning in. We're going up to look at the moon, okay?"

Part of Jean couldn't believe that she was riding in a pickup truck across the dark desert with a woman who actually used the phrase "going steady" and wanted to watch the moon. Another part of her wondered if she would be waking up from the dream anytime soon.

She made a mental note to update her Christmas card list. She wanted to be sure Maryke would have evidence that Jean had taken her advice to open herself to the possibilities with Lea.

They parked on a small hill overlooking the ranch. Jean could see the Hawkins's outside lights glowing yellow below them and in the far distance the faint pale shimmer of Lea's porch light. The moon rose like a phantom, painting the nearby clouds with silver.

Lea opened the door. "Come on, let's get in the back. I've got a couple of blankets."

"Why," Jean asked with amusement, "are we going to sit in the bed of the truck instead of these nice padded seats in the cab?"

She saw Lea's half smile in the moon glow. "Because it's much harder to cuddle in the cab."

When Jean was comfortably settled against Lea in the back of the truck she said, "You know I've never met anyone like you before."

Lea kissed her. "I certainly hope not."

"No, I mean it. Sometimes I can't believe you're real. You really do remind me of one of those old western heroes, always doing the right thing and taking care of everybody around you."

Lea sat back to put some distance between them. "I'm real, Jean. I've got my faults like everybody else, my selfish moments, my doubts and insecurities. I'm a long way from perfect and if you're looking for someone to rescue you, then—"

"I didn't mean it that way," Jean said quickly. "I just wonder if I'll be a disappointment to you. I'm not like you." She sighed. "There are still a lot of things you don't know about me."

Lea drew her close again. "You're right. I don't know your favorite color or the name of the first horse you ever rode or your best subject at school. But those are just facts, Jean. What I do know is that you're brave and tenacious and smart and kind because I've seen those things in you. You make me laugh and I like the way you see the world. I know you're beautiful and I've seen all of you."

Jean smiled in the darkness. "Green," she said. "Roscoe. American History."

"Um, what?"

"Favorite color. First horse. Best subject at school."

Lea laughed. "I'll make a note of that."

"My turn to find out something about you."

"Fire away, Counselor."

Jean reached up and traced the faint scar above Lea's eyebrow. "How did you get this?"

She felt Lea shake with laughter. "I'll bet you were imagining some crazed knife-wielding suspect."

"Something like that," Jean admitted.

"When we were kids, I got in between Loren and my older brother Larry when they were having one of their famous fights. I was trying to stop them. Larry tried to push me out of the way to get to Loren and I fell. I cut my forehead on the edge of a rock."

"I'll bet it bled like crazy."

"Oh, hell yes! I thought my mother was going to kill them both. When she heard me crying she charged out of the house, scooped up Loren to tuck him under one arm and then grabbed Larry by the shirt."

Jean laughed at the picture. "I can just see her."

"She threw one boy in each bedroom and told them to stay there on pain of death. She cleaned me up and if I remember correctly, I got ice cream out of the deal."

They sat in silence for a long time, watching the moon rise slowly. The clouds floated across the face, darkening the glow, then moved off again, their edges catching the light. Jean had always been amazed that the moon held no light of its own, that it only reflected the hidden sun's glory, because tonight it looked like it was shining for them alone. Jean snuggled closer to Lea.

"Are you cold?" Lea asked her softly.

"No. Not with you holding me."

Lea made a contented noise deep in her throat.

All the warmth, all the caring, all the contentment of a home and family seemed to surround Jean like the blanket pulled up to her shoulders.

Jean said suddenly, "Lea, do you love me?"

The silence stretched for so long that Jean began to worry. Finally Lea said, "I was afraid you'd run like a spooked horse if I said anything like that to you this soon."

"Not that long ago I would have run away," Jean admitted. "But I've been rethinking my life quite a bit lately for a lot of reasons. So if you wanted to tell me that, I think you might risk it. If you wanted to."

"Okay, then. I do love you, Jean."

"I'm glad to hear it."

"And why is that?"

"I was planning on falling in love with you sometime around tomorrow, I think," Jean answered. "I just wanted to make sure we were in the same place."

"We are." Lea kissed her.

Jean leaned back into the comforting warmth of Lea's body. She watched the silver moon shine down on the desert darkness.

Bella Books, Inc.

Women. Books. Even Better Together.

P.O. Box 10543
Tallahassee, FL 32302

Phone: 800-729-4992
www.bellabooks.com